THE STILL SMALL VOICE

A CHRISTIAN SPECULATIVE FICTION

LORANA HOOPES

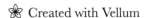

DEDICATION

Dedication Page:

To Brian Johnson, my coach. Thank you for your questions as you inspired this book. And thank you for being my gym family for the last twelve years.

To my teammates who have pushed me and stood by my side over the last ten years. I hope I don't miss anyone.

Brian, Julian, Will, Noah, Dan, Jeremy, Dawn, Nate, Darren, Erik, Alex, Jon, Jonathon, Jesse, Ryann, Lilly, Brandon, Israel, Mike, Sarah, Alex, Chris, Kathy, Jason, Cole, Michelle, Dani, Eric, Stephanie, Brent, Jorge, Anthony, Blake, Jake.

NOTE FROM THE AUTHOR

This book has been a long time coming. It was inspired by a true event, but it took me forever to get it right.

I've been attending the same gym for over a decade. They have become like my family, and they all know that I am a believer. When a girl in our gym and most of her family was tragically killed in a car accident two years ago, it rocked our gym.

Brian stopped me one day and asked me why God allowed bad things to happen to good people? I didn't have an answer for him then. I hadn't even known this girl well, but I spent a lot of time searching and praying. This might not even be the right answer, but what I do know is that God wanted this book written. Even though I kept putting it aside, I kept being reminded of The Still Small

Voice in church services. I knew it was finally time to finish it.

While fiction, there are true elements. You will see that Micah's story is my own. The Prologue is based on my own daughter who said those very words at two. And as some of the characters and places are real, this book is close to my heart.

The book took on a life of its own, and I do have more planned in this series. I hope you'll follow me on this journey even though this isn't my normal romance. There will be some along the way. I hope you enjoy the story and the characters as they are dear to my heart. If you do, please leave a review at your retailer. It really does make a difference because it lets people make an informed decision about books.

Below are books in my small town series. I would love for you to check them out. I'd also like to offer you a sample of my newest book. Free Sample!

The Star Lake series:
When Love Returns

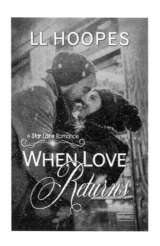

Once Upon A Star

Love Conquers All

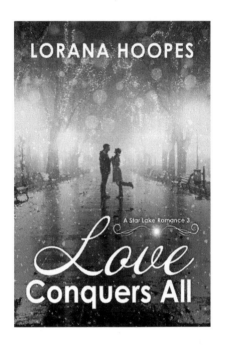

"Kat, honey, what are you doing?" Leah had just laid her two-year old daughter down for the night, but the girl kept tilting her head to look around Leah.

"Trying to see Jesus." Kat smiled matter-of-factly as she looked up at the ceiling. As if this were a common occurrence.

Leah followed her gaze but all she saw was the smoke detector attached to the ceiling. "I don't see anything, honey."

"Jesus is right there, Mommy. Don't you see Him?" Kat's green eyes were wide and round beneath her dark curls.

"I don't honey." Leah tried to keep her voice even as she shook her head. She didn't want her daughter to know she was afraid of her seeing visions. This wasn't the first time she had claimed to see Jesus.

The first time, Jesus had been on the hall ceiling as they were heading out to church.

"Are you ready, munchkin?" Leah scooped up her daughter who giggled as she flew through the air. "You ready to go to church?"

Kat's curls bobbed as she nodded.

"And do you love Jesus?"

Kat's tiny mouth pulled into a large smile and she pointed to the corner of the ceiling. "Uh huh. Hi, Jesus." She waved her little hand, the same way she waved to Leah whenever she dropped her off with the nanny.

Leah brushed it off as a two-year old's imagination. "Do you see Jesus up there?" Kat nodded again and Leah kissed her on the cheek. "Well, that's nice. I wish I could see Jesus like you do."

The second time, Jesus appeared in the corner of Kat's ceiling as Leah was reading her a story.

"Honey, where are you going? The story isn't finished yet."

Leah watched as Kat toddled over to the small area between the closed bedroom door and the closet. She pointed her tiny hand up at the ceiling. "Hi, Jesus." Then she held up her bunny as if offering the stuffed toy to someone. "No?" She lowered the bunny and looked around the room. Then she grabbed a book, returned to the spot, and held it up. "No? Okay." She returned to Leah and climbed back onto her lap to finish the story. "He doesn't want bunny."

Leah forced a tight-lipped smile across her face. Was her

daughter really seeing Jesus or was this the natural young child imagination at work?

Tonight, Jesus was in a different place. He was still on the ceiling but now firmly over the foot of Kat's bed instead of by her bedroom door. While Leah hoped her daughter was seeing Jesus, she couldn't dismiss the possibility that she was seeing something else and that bothered her. "Can you tell me what he looks like?"

"He's wearing white, but He's not talking to Bunny." Kat held up her stuffed bunny – the one that went everywhere with her. Once a soft pink color, time and dirt had worn the plush animal to a dull grey color now.

"Does He talk to you?" Leah supposed she should be relieved that whatever Kat was seeing was wearing white and not black, but the fact he didn't talk struck her as odd. If Kat was seeing Jesus, wouldn't He tell her how much He loved her or something like that? Leah was a religious person. She believed in God, but she'd never seen God or heard Him speak to her.

"He's not talking right now."

"Is He smiling?" She was trying not to ask leading questions, but it was hard with a two-year-old who was just now putting sentences together. Leah wished she could see what her daughter was seeing to make sure it was safe.

"Mommy, who's that?"

Leah followed the tiny index finger pointing to the top of Kat's closet. "I don't know, honey. I don't see anything."

A cold stone settled in Leah's stomach. It was one thing to be seeing Jesus, but now she was seeing something else too? What was wrong with her daughter? She tried to keep the tremor out of her voice as she spoke again. "Here, let's get to sleep. We'll see Jesus in the morning."

She whipped the blanket up and let it fall until it covered Kat completely, another thing Leah found odd. Most of her friends said their children were afraid of the dark, but Kat wanted to be under the blanket. It had to cover her head and her toes. Leah wondered if the visions were why Kat wanted her head covered. Though not simultaneous, they had started at similar times.

Leah sat in the rocker in Kat's room until she heard the rhythmic cadence of breathing signaling her sleep; then she tiptoed out of the room and to the master bedroom down the hall. Her Bible lay on her nightstand, where she kept it to remind her to read every night, and she picked it up before sinking to her knees on the floor.

She clutched the Bible against her chest and turned her head heavenward. "Lord, please protect my daughter. I don't know what she is seeing, but please protect her." That was all Leah could get out before the tears ran down her cheeks. She had waited so long for her baby girl, and now she was terrified that either something was wrong with her or that something would happen to her.

*D*r. Kat Jameson dropped her head into her hands. She hadn't specialized in pediatric oncology for this reason. No one should get cancer, but it was worse when it was a child. Children had their whole life ahead of them, and they came in with small faces and tiny hands. Hands that always seemed to wind their way around Kat's heart.

Thankfully, she'd only had a few child patients in the year she had been practicing on her own, and they had all gone into remission, but this time was different. Cade had brain cancer. It was harder to treat and almost impossible to operate on.

A knock on her door grabbed Kat's attention. She looked up to see Micah Gibson, a fellow doctor at the hospital in her door frame. His blue eyes held more concern than usual as he caught her gaze. "Heard you have a tough case right now."

Kat sighed. "Yeah, a ten-year-old boy whose favorite superhero is Wolverine. I almost wish I could give this kid adamantium, so he could heal himself. Our treatments don't seem to be doing much."

Dr. Gibson cocked an eyebrow as he continued into her small office and sat across from her. "I didn't know you were an X-Men fan."

"That's what you got from my statement?" Kat didn't know the other doctor well, but she hadn't thought he was this insensitive.

His expression softened and he shook his head. "I'm sorry. I was trying to lighten the mood. So, this patient? You've tried everything medically?"

Kat nodded. "Almost. We started with diet because his mom wanted to avoid radiation. When that did nothing, we moved on to proton therapy. He's taking it well, but the tumor just isn't shrinking."

"Have you tried praying?"

His words took her off guard, and she blinked at him. "I didn't realize you were religious."

"I'm not, but I am a Christ follower." He leaned forward, placing his hands on her desk. "I honestly don't know how doctors can see the miracles we see and not believe in God. Can you?"

Kat wasn't sure what to say. She considered herself a

believer though she didn't get to church as often as she once had. Before med school, she had gone every Sunday and even sung in her church choir, but then she'd needed the time to study. When she'd finished med school, she'd had residency which also took up a lot of time. Even now that she was in her own practice, work filled six days of her week, and Sunday was generally her one day off. Still, she attended when she could.

"Anyhow, I'll let you get back to work, but I'll be praying for your patient." Dr. Gibson stood and turned to the door, but before he left, he turned back to Kat. "And you." Then he tapped her door frame and disappeared down the hall.

Prayer. Kat knew she should do more of that, but she'd never seen a prayer answered. And she'd felt no kind of response when she prayed, so it too had fallen to the side. She prayed at church, but that was only because someone on the stage prompted it. And some nights before she fell asleep, but if she were honest, that prayer was more from habit than actually speaking to God. Yes, she should pray more, but right now she needed something else.

A drink. That's what Kat needed. She wasn't a big drinker, more the type to be the designated driver so she could watch other people get silly and stupid, but tonight she needed something. Something to take the edge off. Something to calm her nerves. Something to help clear her head so she didn't have visions of Cade's boyish face haunting her dreams.

Kat turned off her computer and grabbed her purse. She had a few charts to look over, but they could wait another day. Or until Monday.

As she passed the receptionist, Kat paused. A strange feeling that she should thank the woman for something flashed through her thoughts, but she couldn't for the life of her think of what. The woman did a fine job, but nothing exceptional. Chalking it up as nothing important, Kat shook her head and continued out of the hospital and to her car.

Her phone buzzed as she pulled into the parking lot of a nearby bar. Kat swiped the screen and sighed as she read Stella's message.

See you at church tomorrow?

Kat wasn't sure she felt up to church tomorrow. Today had been rough, and if she drank too much, tomorrow morning would be even rougher. However, Stella being her best friend and being Stella, she didn't seem to care that Sunday was Kat's day off. She always reminded Kat of church and when Kat missed too many times, Stella would play the Maddie card. Maddie was Stella's daughter, and she knew Kat would do anything for that strawberry blonde five-year-old.

I'll try. Bad day at work.

Kat shoved the phone back in her purse before Stella

could respond. Stella would not approve of her method of easing the pain and would try to talk her out of going in, but tonight Kat just wanted not to think. She wanted to drown her sorrows and ponder at the cruelty of the universe.

Kat locked her car and walked up the short sidewalk to the front entrance. The peeling paint and faded signage gave her a moment's pause. Could she trust the drinks flowing inside if the exterior of the place was in such need of repair? Deciding she didn't care, Kat gripped the solid handle, pulled the door open, and stepped into the dimly lit establishment.

The bar was mostly empty. A few couples sat in the darkened vinyl booths trading secrets and licentious glances. Kat chose a barstool instead, a few down from the one other bar customer - a portly man perched at the end of the sticky mahogany bar, nursing a beer and probably avoiding going home alone.

Kat signaled the bartender and ordered a Tequila Sunrise. She took a sip and then turned the glass in a slow circle as her thoughts collided in her head.

"You look like you're carrying the weight of the world on those shoulders."

Kat glanced up at the bartender who stared her direction as he wiped a cloth across the bar. Though young, his head was bald, but the hint of color on the sides told her he shaved at least part of it. Somehow, it worked on him. The dimple in his cheek softened the harsh lines of the chiseled face that was still visible under a dark stubble, and his crooked smile gave him an air of jocularity.

Any other night, Kat would have been flattered by his obvious flirtation and might have even left him her number, but tonight she wanted to be left alone. "You could say that." She kept most of the edge out of her voice, though by the bartender's reaction, not enough.

He let out a low whistle, and she forced her eyes back to her drink. Maybe if she ignored him, he would just leave her alone to sate her frustration with the alcohol. Lifting the glass, she tilted her head back and let the remaining liquid burn down her throat.

"When I feel like that, it always helps me to hit things." He had not taken her subtle hint and was now standing in front of her. She could see pale flecks of gold in his hazel eyes.

"How very destructive of you." Her manicured finger tapped the glass as she debated asking for another.

"No, not like that." His laugh was rather melodious and brought a sparkle to his eyes. "I'm a kickboxer, so hitting the bag is cathartic to me. Seems like it might be for you too right now."

Kat kept silent, unsure of what to say, but she let her eyes wander over the rest of his body. He could be a fighter. He had the right build, lean but not too thin and sculpted arms.

"Look, I teach at a gym nearby during the week. Why don't you come by and see if hitting something doesn't give you some reprieve from whatever you're feeling?" He slipped a white card out of his pocket and slid it across the bar to her.

She held his gaze another moment before dropping her eyes to the card. It was white with black lettering, simple but still eye-catching with the black boxing gloves gracing the corner. "The Academy of Brian Johnson?"

"I know, not the most original name. I didn't name it, the owner did, but it's a good work out. Bring that card in, and I'll make sure you get a week for free to try it out."

"Thanks, I'll think about it." Kat pocketed the card and then pushed her glass forward. "Can I get another?"

The man's eyebrow rose as he regarded her with narrowed eyes, but he pulled out the tequila bottle and filled her glass again.

When the second glass was empty, Kat pushed a twenty across the bar and stood to leave. However, the room spun and she grabbed the counter for support.

"Hey, I don't think you should be driving. Let me call you a cab."

Kat focused on the bartender and took a deep breath. The room righted itself and she pulled her shoulders back and held up a hand. "I'm fine. I don't live far. Thank you for the drinks." Before he could say anything else, Kat made her way to the exit cursing her low tolerance.

The cool night air sobered her a little more and Kat remembered she had eaten nothing since lunch. No wonder two drinks were hitting her so hard. Thankfully, she always kept a few granola bars in her car as she often missed dinner and had to eat on the run. She'd eat one and sit in the car until she felt able to drive. While she lived nearby, she had no intention of causing an accident or getting a DUI. Either could ruin her career.

She climbed into the car, but didn't start the engine. Leaning over, Kat popped open the glove compartment and snatched a bar, peeling back the wrapper and taking a large bite. Then she fished in her purse for her phone. Might as well see what Stella said in response.

Want to pray about it?

Kat chuckled at the irony. What was it with everyone and prayer today?

~

"This is the one God has chosen?" Afriel asked his superior. He was still learning the gauntlet of how to navigate the world of mortals and how to avoid the demons.

Galadriel's smile was soft, as if he knew Afriel wasn't questioning him, just trying to learn all he could. "God has plans for Kat. He has since she was little, but she has not been open to listening to Him since her father left. Maybe she will be now."

"How can that be?" Afriel asked. "Isn't she a Christian? Doesn't she believe in God?"

Galadriel smiled, but sadness laced it. "There are many who call themselves Christians, and even more who believe in God, but few of them take the time to seek His voice. Perhaps if they did, things could be different."

SATURDAY MORNING IN LUBBOCK TEXAS

*J*ordan Wright's eyes popped open. For the fifth straight night in a row, the same woman had invaded her dream. Unsure of what else to do, Jordan crawled out of bed and collapsed to her knees. She folded her hands together and lowered her head to rest on them. Her blond hair fell on either side obscuring her peripheral vision. She had no idea what words to say, so she closed her eyes and let her heart speak for itself, begging the Lord to explain the dreams or else to make them stop. She could no longer pass them off as coincidences or hallucinations. There was apparently some reason for their nightly appearance.

As the silence pressed in, Jordan fought the urge to open her eyes. The pastor had spoken recently about listening for the still, small voice. Jordan was determined to give it a little longer, to really listen, though the silence unnerved her.

"Tell her." Though not audible, the words caressed Jordan and she understood them all the same. She opened her eyes, still unsure exactly what she was supposed to be doing, but sure of where she needed to go.

After showering and dressing, Jordan drove the short distance to Indiana Avenue Baptist church. It was not Sunday, but the woman she sought worked in the church, and she was certain she would be there.

As she parked the car, the enormity of what she was about to do hit her. What if she was wrong? What if it was only her imagination? The hesitant thoughts caused her to pause outside the church doors, her hand on the silver handle, but then the woman's face flashed in front of her eyes like a silent movie, and Jordan swallowed her trepidation and pulled open the door.

Jordan turned left toward the offices amazed at how quiet the church was. On Sundays, groups of people milled about in the foyer between services munching on the provided muffins as they caught up on their struggles and accomplishments. Today though the hall was empty and the hum of the air conditioning was the only audible sound.

Another left down the short hallway that housed the offices brought her outside Cathy's door. She tugged on her shirt, still a little snug on the body that hadn't regained its pre-pregnancy shape. Though her heart galloped in her chest, she took a deep breath and raised her hand to knock on the wooden door.

The door swung open, and Cathy's warm brown eyes regarded her from the other side. "Jordan? What brings you here today?"

Jordan blinked, taken off guard for a moment that Cathy knew her name. They had only been introduced once, and though Cathy had come to some of the college meetings, Jordan hadn't thought the woman would remember her. "I was hoping I could talk to you for a minute," she said, recovering. "That is if you're not too busy."

A smile spread across Cathy's face. "I'm always busy, but never too busy to listen." She opened the door farther and stepped back, gesturing with her left arm to the small office inside.

Jordan crossed the threshold and stopped, unsure whether to sit in a chair or stay standing. Deciding to stand, she clasped her hands together to keep them from displaying the shaking she felt radiating through her core.

"I hope you don't think I'm crazy," she began, looking up into Cathy's expectant eyes, "but I feel the Lord is speaking to me. I believe I'm supposed to tell you not to be discouraged and that you are on the right track."

Cathy's eyes widened, and her hand rose to cover her mouth. Her eyes bored into Jordan's as if searching for the truth. Then they filled with tears and she smiled. "Oh, praise the Lord. I don't know how you knew, but you've just given me the answer I've been seeking for months." She pulled Jordan in for a fierce hug.

"You're welcome," Jordan stammered, taken aback by the response. "If I may though, what does the pastor have to be discouraged about? I haven't attended many, but this church seems genuine and all the people are really nice."

Cathy smiled, but it was a small, sad smile as if she had secret knowledge of the discouragement her husband faced first hand. "You'd be surprised how much discourages him, but this wasn't about my husband. It was about me. Recently, I've taken over the women's ministry and seen a decrease in attendance at our events. I thought perhaps I was mistaken thinking God had wanted me to head it and was about to tell the board to find a new leader. I'd been praying for guidance for the last few months and now here you are. May I ask how you knew?"

Jordan shook her blond mane. "I doubt you'll believe me, but I'll tell you." Cathy motioned to the brown chairs and the two women sat down. "A few weeks ago, I gave my son up for adoption." The image of the first vision after she met Amanda flashed through her mind and Jordan blinked and shook her head. "Actually, it goes back farther than that. Last year, someone raped me at a frat party."

A small audible gasp escaped from Cathy's lips before

her hand could cover them completely, but Jordan continued.

"I ended up pregnant, and I thought it was the worst day of my life. Eighteen and pregnant. I was afraid to tell my mom, and when I did, she pushed me to terminate the pregnancy. I figured it would be the easiest way out, but for some reason I kept putting it off. The day I decided to go through with it, I met Amanda Adams at a fair on campus. She didn't know about the baby, but we shared some weird connection and she told me my baby mattered. It was like time froze and the surrounding sounds muted. When I returned to my dorm room, a vision of my son filled my mind, and I knew I couldn't go through with the abortion.

"I wasn't religious, but the day I put him in another woman's arms and left the hospital without him, this empty ache consumed me. It was definitely the most difficult thing I've ever done, but I'm still glad I chose life for him. However, the emptiness didn't go away. I kept looking for something to fill the void and I remembered Amanda's invite to church. I came with her here and a few days after that I asked God into my heart."

The dark-haired woman across from her smiled and Jordan continued.

"I still didn't feel complete though, so I asked God to show me how I could help. That's when the visions started. At first, they were just feelings like an urge to read a certain passage if I had a question, but a few days ago, I saw your face. I didn't know what He wanted me to do at first, but when I was finally quiet, I heard the still, small voice. I'm sure I must sound crazy."

"On the contrary." Cathy offered a wide smile. "You have the gift of prophecy."

"The gift of what?" Jordan's brow furrowed. She had never heard about this gift.

"Prophecy," Cathy repeated. "There are several spiritual gifts discussed in the Bible, and we all have one or more of them. Some of us feel them more strongly than others and some of us just haven't had our heart opened to know what ours is, but it sounds like yours is the gift of prophecy. You can hear God's words and relay them to people who need to hear them, like me. Perhaps, you'll even be able to tell people what might happen if they don't change their ways. Here, come with me, I think we have a book in the library that might help you out."

Jordan followed Cathy, still struggling to make sense of a gift of prophecy. She was no one. Why would He give her such an amazing gift?

Cathy opened a door that led to a closet-sized room, teeming with books. Jordan's eyes widened at the sheer volume of books in the tiny room. She hadn't even known the church had a library, and yet here was a room with nothing but bookshelves on every wall, and each shelf was filled with books. Cathy tapped a finger against her lips as her eyes scanned the shelves. She turned from one bookshelf to face another and ran her finger across the outer spines of the books. "Ah, here we go." She pulled out a small five by eight paperback.

Jordan accepted the book and stared at the cover. God's Gifts and How to Use Them by Dr. George Herman. "This will help me?" She looked back to Cathy, her eyes seeking reassurance.

"I think so. It's been a while since I read it, but I remember it helping me figure out that my gift was the gift of helping. Even when I was little, I remember always wanting to help people with problems, but when I got to college, I wondered what use I really was to God. I was often too quiet to approach people though I wanted to. A friend showed me this book, and it really opened my eyes. I saw that helping was my gift and that by not approaching people and offering help when I could that I was grieving God. It gave me the courage to speak out."

Though she still had her doubts, Cathy's brown eyes were so sincere that Jordan felt she should at least give the book a chance. "Thank you," she said, tucking the book to her chest, "but why would God choose me? I'm nobody. I didn't even believe in Him until a month ago."

Cathy smiled. "Sometimes it is because we are humble and broken that God chooses us. You see if He chooses someone unlikely, then when His will is done, people can see that it is only because of God and not because of the person, but you aren't nobody, Jordan. You are God's wonderful creation, and He has a purpose for you."

When Jordan returned to her apartment, she curled up on the couch and cracked the book open. She had never been the biggest book worm—relying more on her good looks and her charm—but this book spoke to her. As she read the words, images from the last few weeks jumped to mind and she realized she had been receiving little signs she hadn't even caught. Amazed, she continued to turn the pages, eager to learn more though she still had no idea why God would choose her to bestow such a gift upon.

~

"Wait, she's who he's choosing to use? Why her? She's so far away; isn't there anyone closer?"

Galadriel shook his head as he watched Jordan on the bed. "She is perfect for many reasons. First, because of what Cathy said. She is unexpected so God will be glorified. Second, she herself has a gift and that will enable Kat to accept her gift quicker. Third, though a lot of people claim to follow Jesus, few sadly take the time to talk to him and learn of their gifts. Humans have become too attached to their technology and other items to keep their minds busy. They have forgotten the most important things–to read and study God's word daily and to listen for the still, small voice."

The younger angel shook his mane of golden hair. "How can they not know what we know? See what we see?"

"Very few of them have faith strong enough. Though many more used to believe, now most need to see something or hear something, but they are not focused enough to see it or hear it when it does happen. But Jordan is listening, and Kat will soon too."

SUNDAY, WASHINGTON

"Glad you could make it." Stella's warm smile was the same, but a paleness covered her face that wasn't normally there.

Kat swallowed her irritation and hugged her friend. "I try to make it every Sunday I can, but sometimes work gets in the way."

"Aunt Kat!" Maddie's excited voice carried down the hallway, and a moment later her free hand wrapped around Kat's leg. She clenched a muffin tightly in her other hand.

"Hey, Maddiecakes!" Kat reached down and hugged the slender girl.

"I simply worry that work is getting in the way more often." Stella was intent on continuing the previous conversation. Even the added distraction of Maddie and Patrick, who appeared a moment later, didn't sway her.

He shot an apologetic look at them both before bending down to Maddie's level. "Maddie, we don't run in church, remember?"

Maddie nodded and looked adequately remorseful. "Sorry, Dad, I was just excited to see Aunt Kat."

"Good morning, Kat." Patrick's tone always came across stiff and forced to her.

"Morning."

Stella shook her head and her blond curls bounced against her shoulders. "Never mind. We can talk after church. Will you come over for lunch?"

"Sure." Kat had other things she needed to be doing like laundry and shopping, but Stella had asked in front of Maddie. The girl's eyes had lit up at the question and Kat knew there was no way Maddie would let her say no.

"Come on, Maddie. Let's get you to class. You can visit with Aunt Kat after church."

Maddie frowned up at Patrick, but took his hand and followed him down a separate hallway to her Sunday school class. Stella and Kat continued into the sanctuary. The music was just starting as they claimed their seats, and the two women joined in the singing. Patrick arrived a moment later and snagged a seat next to Stella.

When the music ended, the pastor took the stage. "We don't always remind you, but we have an open altar here.

As we go into prayer, if you would like to come down and pray at the altar, you are welcome. If you need more prayer, please let us know and one of our pastors will pray with you. Will you pray with me now? Lord -"

He continued, but Kat didn't hear the rest as Stella scooting past her to move to the altar consumed her focus. What was she doing? What on earth could she need more prayer about? Stella had the perfect life - a great husband, even if he was a little stiff for Kat, and a wonderful daughter.

"What is she doing?" Kat made sure her voice was low as she leaned over to Patrick.

"You'll have to ask her." Then he stood and followed Stella to the altar, leaving Kat alone in her seat.

Kat bit her lip as she watched her two friends kneel up front. Should she join them? Praying in front of people had never been her strength, nor did she want to pray with the congregation staring at her. Plus, she had no idea what she'd say. *Go Pray with her.* The words were a feeling more than a thought, but Kat ignored them anyway. People would look at her exactly as she was looking at Stella now and wonder what she needed prayer for. And Kat didn't want that. So, she stayed in her seat looking almost as conspicuous there as she would have been up front at the carpeted area.

When the prayer time ended, Stella and Patrick returned to the aisle. Kat opened her mouth to question

Stella, but the pastor began the sermon then, and Kat was forced to keep her question to herself until the sermon ended.

Though she tried to stay focused on the words of the pastor, Kat's mind kept wandering. She wondered how Cade was doing; she made a list of items she needed to pick up at the grocery store; and she tried to visualize her schedule to see what the next week held.

Next to her, Stella wrote furiously in a little book. When she wasn't writing, her eyes were glued to the man up front and Kat wondered when she had become such a fanatic. Stella, like herself, had grown up in the church, and she had always seemed a bit more dedicated, but she had never seemed as focused as she did now. What had happened to her the last few weeks?

"Want to tell me what that was about?" Kat asked Stella as they packed up after the service.

"What do you mean?" Stella tucked her Bible into her large purse and slung it over her shoulder.

"The altar call and then the note taking."

Stella shrugged. "I felt the need to pray." She stated the words matter-of-factly as if they made all the sense in the world.

"But you can pray at your seat. Why go down there where everyone can see you?"

Stella stopped and stared at Kat for a moment. "I don't care if people see me. My praying isn't for them;

it's for God. Haven't you ever gotten a stirring in your soul? Some need to do something even though you don't know why?"

Kat was about to shake her head no when she remembered feeling like she should have gotten up and prayed with Stella. Plus, there was that moment yesterday with the receptionist. Was that what Stella was talking about? "I don't know. I guess I'm not sure."

Stella's eyes turned sad. "What happened to you, Kat? When did you start drifting away?"

"What do you mean? I'm here as often as I can be."

Stella shook her head. "That's not what I mean. You used to be on fire for God. You wouldn't have cared if people saw you praying. In high school when you rededicated your life, you said you wanted God to use you."

"What?" Kat had no memory of this. Or if she did, she had blocked it out.

"Yeah, don't you remember? That night at the retreat. You went down front and prayed. Then you told me that you felt God was calling you to do something big."

A scoffing noise escaped Kat's throat as the two walked toward the exit. "I was eighteen, Stella. I thought everything in my life would be big."

"That's not what you meant, Kat and you know it." Stella paused as Patrick and Maddie came down the hall. "Come over for lunch. We need to finish this conversation.

Kat nodded and followed Stella and her family outside, but as she got in her car, she couldn't stop thinking about this change in Stella. Stella was fun and lighthearted, but today she seemed much more serious.

Even over lunch. Though she wore a bright smile and carried on the conversation, Kat watched as Stella ate less than normal and often pushed her food around on her plate to give the impression she was eating.

"What is going on with you?" Kat asked as they cleared the table after lunch.

Stella looked to the backyard where Patrick had taken Maddie to play. A sad, wistful smile crossed her lips before she sucked in a breath and turned to Kat. "I've been having headaches. I went down to the altar today because I felt called to pray for my health."

Stella's words hit Kat like a ton of bricks, and she sank into a chair. In all the time she'd known Stella, she'd never known her to have headaches. Not even once. "Have you been to the doctor?"

Stella joined her at the table. "I have, and they found nothing wrong, but I'm seeing a specialist this week. It's more than that though Kat. Don't you feel it?"

"Feel what?" Fear crept up Kat's spine.

"The end. I feel like it's coming soon."

"Don't talk like that. I'm sure it's nothing, and the specialist will find out what it is."

"No, Kat. I didn't mean like that. I mean like end of

days. Look around. The world is upside down and people are at each other's throats. Even churches have blurred the lines on what is acceptable behavior."

Kat shrugged. "I guess I hadn't thought about it much." She hadn't noticed at all actually, but if she told Stella that, she'd be in for another lecture.

Stella leaned across the table. "I know, and that's what worries me. You have done nothing much. Are you still reading the Bible? Do you even pray anymore?"

Kat opened her mouth to protest and defend herself, but then closed it. She couldn't remember the last time she'd read her Bible and other than her obligatory prayer each night, she couldn't remember another time she'd prayed either. "Okay, so I have a little work to do, but what's gotten into you?"

A peaceful smile lit Stella's face. "I started listening. You know how the pastor's been speaking about hearing the Holy Spirit and that still, small voice? Well, I devoted time to really listening, and I feel him, Kat."

Kat's brow arched on her forehead. She wanted to believe Stella, but she couldn't remember ever feeling God or the Holy Spirit talking to her. Nor did she have time to just sit and listen for a voice that might or might not come.

"Promise me, Kat, that you'll try to listen. Take some time to pray and focus before it's too late."

"I've got plenty of time, Stella. I'm only thirty-two."

"How can you say that? You work with cancer patients all day, Kat. How many of them had their time cut short?"

Kat wanted to argue with her, but Stella was right. Cade Jackson was the perfect example of that. "Okay, fine. I promise I'll try."

Though Stella nodded, Kat could tell she was still troubled. However, she let the matter die and moved to lighter topics. Kat couldn't help but breathe a sigh of relief.

When she returned home that evening, the promise flashed in her mind and Kat went in search of her Bible. She found it hiding under other books on her nightstand. A light layer of dust coated the top, and a tiny pang of guilt pierced her as she dusted it away. It had been awhile since she had read.

Unsure where to start, she let the Bible fall open and landed in Psalms. She read a few chapters and then closed the book. "Okay, God, I'm waiting."

Kat sat in silence for a few minutes, but she still felt nothing. No words, no feelings, just the need to go over work for tomorrow. And the reminder she still hadn't stopped at the grocery store or started her laundry. With a sigh, Kat opened her eyes. Maybe one day she would feel whatever it was Stella was feeling, but it would not be today.

～

"*How* ow could she not hear that?" Afriel's eyebrows rose as he turned to face Galadriel.

"Humanity has changed. It is busier now and there are more distractions. Few take the time to really listen even when they speak to God." Galadriel's face held a sadness. "I will see what the next orders are. I fear it may take something much bigger to get her attention."

"Like what?"

"Whatever it is, it will be in His plan."

MONDAY, TEXAS

*J*ordan paused, the brush halfway through her hair. A face flashed before her eyes—a girl with mousy brown hair and sad eyes hiding behind glasses. Though vaguely familiar, Jordan could not place where she knew the girl. "I will need a little more to go on God."

The brush continued its course through her blond hair as she waited for more information. This was only her second vision, but she had expected it would come with at least as much information as the first had. However, by the time she finished getting ready for class, she had received nothing more than the girl's face and two words—she matters.

Deciding to keep her eyes open, she slung her bag over

her shoulder and headed to class. Her year had not started off well, but as she crossed the campus to Holden Hall, Jordan could honestly say she was happy with where her life was at now. Giving up her son had been hard, but the parents had agreed to an open adoption and Jordan knew one day she would get to tell her son that she loved him.

It hadn't been easy staying caught up in class either. Even though it was college, people still whispered and pointed at her. Plus, she had to miss days occasionally due to fatigue or appointments. And of course, there had been a few days in the hospital when she delivered, but Jordan had pushed through. After her finals today, her Sophomore year would be over. That alone was reason to rejoice.

As she neared the steps, her phone buzzed in her pocket. Jordan dropped her eyes to her pocket as she pulled it out, but there was no text or call. The screen was dark. After swiping a finger across the screen to illuminate it, she checked both the messages and the phone icon but neither showed a missed message.

"Well, that's weird." The words were soft, under her breath. Then she shook her head and pocketed the phone again. Her feet stepped before her eyes lifted from her pocket and she slammed into another body. "I'm sorry." As she stepped back and looked up, her breath caught in her throat. The face before her belonged to the girl from her vision. "It's you." Breathless and barely more than a whisper, the words didn't even catch the other girl's attention.

"I'm sorry. You probably didn't see me." The girl pushed her glasses up and dropped her head, focusing on the ground. Her brown hair covered her face like a curtain.

Jordan stared at her. Was the girl apologizing? Realizing the girl was waiting for her to speak or move, Jordan blinked and found her voice. "No, I'm sorry. I didn't see you, but it was my fault. However, I'm glad I ran into you as I was looking for you."

The girl's head lifted, her eyebrows arching as her eyes widened. "You were looking for me? Why?"

Jordan glanced at her watch, hoping she had a few minutes to spare before her test. Twenty minutes. It wasn't as long as she hoped, but it would have to be long enough. "To tell you that you matter."

The girl blinked at her a moment and then she turned her head as if looking for something or someone. She probably thought Jordan was playing a cruel joke on her and there was a camera somewhere catching it all on film. Finally, her skin paled and she leaned closer Jordan. "How did you know?"

Jordan shrugged, and her lips formed into a lopsided smile. "I can tell you, but I doubt you'll believe me." She motioned with her head to the cement lip surrounding the side of the building and the girl followed her, sitting down next to Jordan, eyes still wide, expectant. "I saw you in a vision." Jordan hoped the girl wouldn't think she was crazy. "I think God is using me to speak to people, and He told me to tell you that you matter."

The stare from the girl was blank, unreadable, and Jordan bit her lip to keep from asking what she thought. Then the girl's eyes filled with moisture, spilling over and streaking down her cheeks in succession. Again, Jordan wanted to say something, to comfort the girl, but something told her to wait. A few students shot them a questioning glance as they passed, but none approached them.

"You don't understand how much I needed to hear those words," the girl finally said, wiping the wetness from her cheeks. "I thought college would be great, but I'm so far from my family, and I have made no friends. No one ever seems to notice me. I was contemplating dropping out and going home. In fact, I was coming early to tell Professor Davis I would skip the final, but he wasn't in his office."

"Professor Davis? Are you in Econ 202?" A sickening feeling erupted in Jordan's stomach as she asked, knowing the answer before the girl nodded. She had been in Jordan's class all semester, and yet she hadn't been able to place her when she saw the vision. How many times had she ignored this girl's sad eyes and walked right past her? "I'm sorry-" The pause drew out as Jordan waited for the girl to provide her name.

"Julie," the girl offered, picking up on the hint.

Jordan smiled. "I'm sorry, Julie, that I never got to know you this semester, but if you're up for it, I would like to now. Well, after our test that is."

Julie sniffed, wiped a hand across her nose, and then smiled. The effect transformed her face, and for the first time, Jordan saw a tiny sparkle light in her eye. "I'd like that."

As the two girls walked into the hall together, Jordan couldn't help but wonder how many other people she had missed. How many other Julies were out there just waiting for someone to acknowledge them?

"Why is she so different? So able to hear God's voice?" Afriel wanted to be of more help, but he was struggling with how different all these humans were.

"She asked for God to use her. He has this gift to bestow on many. He is simply waiting for them to ask."

"Why do they not pay attention to each other? Why did no one reach out to this girl?"

"Distractions. Diversions. Those are just some of the tools the demons use to keep them from listening and following God."

Afriel nodded, but sadness still filled his face.

MONDAY, WASHINGTON

*K*at glanced at her watch as she locked the car door. Shoot. She was late. How did that even happen? She lived alone, so there was no one she had to wait on, and she'd left the same time this morning that she did every morning. Then she remembered her quick detour to a nearby coffee shop. There had been no creamer in the fridge this morning, and she didn't drink black coffee. She had planned on skipping it, but a desire for a caramel macchiato had overwhelmed her. Now, she was seven minutes late.

Kat quickened her pace, adjusting her bag as she went. The hospital doors slid open and she made her way to the elevator, punching the button for the oncology floor.

Her heart slowed as she stepped off on her floor. Thankfully, she didn't have a patient first thing this morning. She stopped at the receptionist's desk just long enough to realize it was not the normal woman. "Where's the regular girl?"

The blond head lifted to reveal a young woman with wide eyes and a frazzled expression. "Um, I don't know. I just got the call to be here today." She shuffled papers on the desk but proceeded only in making a mess.

Kat shook her head and continued to her office. Why was it so hard to find good help these days? She had just dropped her bag on the floor when she heard a voice at her door.

"Did you remember to pray about it?"

Micah Gibson leaned once again on her door frame again. What was with this guy? He had worked here for a month and she generally only passed him in the hallways. They exchanged a wave, maybe a smile, but no full-blown conversation. Now, he had come to her office twice seeking her out. While he was nice to look at with his chiseled features and bright blue eyes, Kat had no interest in dating at work. That was one lesson she learned early in life.

"Um, no." She opened the laptop and hit the power button. "I meant to, but I got a little busy with the rest of my life." Why did she feel like she needed to defend her actions to him?

His frank gaze held hers a moment as if he were trying to decide if she were lying or not. "It only takes a minute to pray. You could do it now."

"Yes, I suppose I could." A hint of ice existed in her tone, and she waited for him to leave, but he continued to stare at her.

"Did you get stuck in the accident on Pacific?"

"What?" Kat really needed to get to work and he was distracting her.

"There was an accident this morning. I figured that's why you were late."

"No, I stopped to get a coffee. I guess it's a good thing or I might have been caught in the accident."

He stared at her a moment longer. "Yes, I guess it was. Well, I better get to work as well. I'll keep praying for your patient."

"Thanks." As he left the office, Kat wondered how he had known she took Pacific to work. Had she mentioned it? She didn't think she had, but she must have for him to know. Maybe he had overheard a conversation she had with someone else. Yes, that must be it.

With the distraction gone, Kat sat down and pulled up her work for the day. She had a few patients to check on today including Cade. With a sigh, Kat decided she should start with him.

She walked down the hall to where the treatment rooms were. Patients rarely had to stay long, but Cade would receive another proton treatment today.

When she entered his room, surprise filled her at his

altered appearance. He looked chipper and not as pale. "Hey, bud, feeling better today?"

He nodded and grinned before returning his attention to his tablet.

"He woke up hungry today for the first time in a long time. Does that mean it's working?" Hope glistened in his mother's eyes and threaded her voice.

"It might." Kat was hesitant to give her false hope. She'd seen too many patients have a good day or even a week, think they were cured, and then succumb to the cancer shortly after. "But remember that some days are better than others. I'll ask for another scan today after his treatment. That should tell us more."

"Thank you." The woman placed a hand on Kat's arm for just a moment and then it returned to the chain around her neck. Before her fingers closed completely over the object, Kat made out the shape of a small golden cross.

"You're welcome. Cade, I'll see you soon."

He flashed her a thumb up sign, still too engrossed in his game to look up. It was nice to see him acting like a normal ten-year-old again.

The rest of her day flew by, and as Kat packed up, she realized she was done before five for once. She could get a work out in. In fact, she might even try the gym the bartender had suggested. Kat was fairly certain the card still sat in her car's cupholder where she'd placed it Saturday evening.

She locked her office door and headed toward the elevator.

"Wait. Dr. Jameson?"

Kat turned back to the receptionist who looked even more frazzled than she had this morning.

"I meant to give this to you earlier." She held out a message slip.

"Thank you." As Kat took the paper, she hoped it wasn't important. Maybe she should have thanked the regular receptionist on Saturday. At least she always got Kat her messages in a timely manner.

The message was short. A potential client. Kat would return the call in the morning. After tucking the paper inside her bag, she continued to the elevator. With no further interruptions, she was back at her car minutes later.

The card was indeed still in her car, and with fifteen minutes until four, Kat thought she could make it in time to try a class.

As she pulled into the parking lot of the large white building though, she wondered what she was doing. Boxing had never been her thing; she was more of a yoga girl. But the more she had thought about the bartender's words, the more she wondered if hitting something might be cathartic for her. It certainly couldn't hurt. She grabbed the bag of workout clothes she had packed just in case, locked her car, and headed for the entrance.

Taking a deep breath and pulling her shoulders back, she grasped the cool metal handle and pulled it toward her. The room inside was like a giant warehouse. Rows of blue and red bags hung from chains near the back of the room. A few guys were interspersed among the bags, throwing punches or kicks. The resulting thudding sound echoed throughout the large room.

On the far right, a shelving unit housed a plethora of padded gear and a large black boxing ring took up one corner. A mirror covered part of the wall at the front of the room. To the left was a desk. The man from the bar the other night sat behind it eating a granola bar. His bare feet were propped on the desk. A pair of black shorts and a black t-shirt made up his uniform, if you could call it that.

Kat took a step in his direction. Though padded in what looked like a type of foam, the floor had little give beneath her feet.

He looked up as she neared, pulling his feet off the desk and standing. His hazel eyes sparkled as a smile stretched across his face. One tooth on his bottom row was slightly crooked, but charming. "Hey, you came."

Kat shrugged. "I had nothing else to do tonight."

"Well, that's a start," he said with a laugh. "Let me show you around. He led her past a row of chairs lining the far-left wall. A lone girl occupied one chair, wrapping a colored fabric around her wrists. "Bathrooms." He pointed to two individual rooms along the back wall. "They're labeled men and women, but they're single stalls so you can use whichever one you want. Weight room. It's small, but it works."

Kat popped her head in the open doorway of the room he pointed to. Not much equipment, but she didn't use them much anyway. She hurried to catch up to him as he continued along the back wall. A half wall jutted out and water bottles and gloves sat along it. At the end, a doorway opened to the left.

"This is the locker room. You can leave your stuff in here. There's a locker if you want, but bring your own lock, and there are three changing rooms right there. We don't wear shoes when we kickbox as you can see." He pointed to his bare feet and wiggled his toes. "There's also a treadmill and an elliptical right outside, but we do most of our work on the bags."

"Okay." Kat nodded hoping she would remember everything he had spouted at her. "Shall I get changed then?"

"You bet. I'm Jason by the way." He stuck out his hand, and after a moment, Kat took it and returned the shake.

"I'm Kat."

"Oh, I almost forgot. Do you have gloves?"

Kat shook her head. She figured she would need them eventually but hadn't stopped to get any yet. No sense buying a pair if she found out this workout wasn't for her.

"No problem, we have spares, but I have to warn you that you'll want to wash your hands after. A lot of people have used them."

Kat wrinkled her nose in disgust, eliciting a laugh from Jason before he turned his lanky frame to the exit and passed out of sight. Sighing, she set her bag down on one of the wooden benches and fished out her clothes. *Here goes nothing.*

A few minutes later, changed and fighting a feeling of self-consciousness, Kat exited the locker room back into the main room. An older man with a head full of salt and pepper hair called the class to order. His sleeveless shirt showed off his well-toned arms and his legs beneath his shorts sported many tattoos. *He must be the owner.* Kat joined the few people in a line near the bags feeling conspicuous and out of place. The man at the front bowed to Jason, who returned the bow and then yelled, "Run the bags."

Kat's uncertainty lasted only a moment as the rest of the people in the line began circling the bags in a loose formation. Though not much of a runner, Kat's lean body joined the chorus of people creating an imaginary square around the hanging bags. The foam floor felt funny beneath her bare feet, and a few times her toe snagged on the foam floor and she stumbled forward, catching herself just before falling and making a fool of herself.

The run seemed to go on forever, but finally Jason uttered the blessed word "stop" and the class began stretching. **This** Kat could do well. Her dedication to yoga ensured her flexibility, and she enjoyed the feeling of her muscles stretching. She was amazed as she stretched at how limber Jason was as well. He could do a full front split and lean forward so his elbows were on the ground.

When the stretching time ended, he appeared by her side holding out a pair of black boxing gloves. "I tried to find the driest pair I could for you."

Her forehead wrinkled as she took the gloves. They didn't feel wet to her until she slid her hand inside. Then the cold damp feeling of old sweat covered her hand, and she shivered. If she ever came back, she would have to buy her own gloves first. This was not an experience she wanted to repeat.

Jason stood watching her, a knowing smile on his face. "Don't worry, once you add your own, it won't feel so bad." His eyes twinkled, and though disgusted, Kat couldn't help but smile back.

He then led her and a few others to some bags near the back and walked them through the punches and kicks. One, a jab with your left hand. Two, a cross with your right. Three, a hook with your left. Four, a hook with your right. Kat found the numbers confusing until Jason explained that odd numbers were thrown from the left side and even from the right. At least if you were right handed. If you were left handed, then the opposite was true.

Once she had the numbers down, Kat could focus on the feel of her hand connecting with the bag. Though she was sure she wasn't doing it exactly right, the resounding thud when she hit the heavy bag did seem to take the edge off her anger.

When the hour was over, Kat was drenched in sweat and sure she would be sore the next few days, but her shoulders felt a little lighter. After removing the now even sweatier gloves, she handed them back to Jason, who smiled and raised his eyebrow at her.

"How was your first workout?"

"It was good. I can see why you do it. It felt good to hit something."

"It always does. You coming back then?"

Kat tilted her head at him, curious if he was asking just from a business standpoint or if he might have an interest in her. Deciding she'd be fine either way, she nodded. "Yeah, I think I will."

He grinned and nodded, and Kat returned to the locker room to gather her things. She looked around for a shower but realized there was none. Oh, well, she had nothing planned for the evening. She could shower at home.

After slinging her bag with her work clothes in it over

her shoulder, Kat exited the building feeling a little less like an outsider. She unlocked her car and flung the bag on the passenger seat. She'd have to tell Stella about this and see if she'd be up for a workout. They'd often worked out together before Maddie was born and Kat's schedule grew too hectic. But that could wait for tomorrow. Tonight, she just wanted to shower and curl up with a glass of wine.

TUESDAY, TEXAS

ordan pinched her eyes shut, wanting the face to disappear. "Oh, Lord, please don't make me do that. That is not my forte at all." She waited for a voice or a different vision, but the face remained. It was the face of the blond girl she had met at the gym just the other day. Krissy something or other, but it wasn't the face that bothered her as much as the message she was supposed to deliver.

Though her visions were still new, they had all been positive messages, delivering hope or peace to someone. Jordan suddenly felt like Jonah in the Bible and understood why he had run from Nineveh the first time. Who wanted to be the bearer of news like this?

"I don't even know her well, Lord. Why would she even listen to me?" She waited, hoping it would change, but instead all the sordid details flooded her mind. Everything she would need to convince the woman she was telling the truth appeared before her eyes. Names, faces, dates. Details she should have no way of knowing.

"Show her the truth." Jordan felt the voice more than heard it, and she knew better than to argue any longer.

Cathy's words from the first day echoed in her head "Perhaps you might even be able to tell people what will happen if they don't change their ways." It was the best she could hope for. Maybe Krissy would believe her and change her ways because the path Jordan had seen looked like it would be a painful one to walk.

As Jordan passed through the single pane door to the gym, her throat dried up like water in a desert. She pleaded again silently for her task to change but her only answer was another flash of Krissy's face. Swallowing her fear, she scanned her member badge and headed to the locker room.

She hadn't come to work out, but with no idea when Krissy would arrive, she felt the need to release some of the pent-up energy rolling around in her stomach. Plus, she would look less conspicuous in workout attire. After stripping off her street clothes and changing into work out gear, Jordan locked her items in a locker and pinned the key to her shirt.

As she exited the locker room, she glanced around the room for Krissy, hoping she wasn't here yet. To the left was the weight room, which Jordan seldom frequented. She enjoyed lifting, but the dedicated weight room was where the power lifters hung out.

The one and only time she had tried it, she had left feeling embarrassed about her thirty-pound curls as the men in the room had all been curling over a hundred. To their credit, they had said nothing to her or even shot her disparaging looks. But, the discomfort had surfaced none the less and Jordan decided if she wanted to lift, she could use the small weight rack in the main room.

Straight ahead was the large room where group classes were held, but none of them started for another hour, so Jordan knew Krissy wouldn't be there. That only left the cardio room to the right. Rows of elliptical machines, treadmills, and bikes filled this area along with a weight circuit course and the small rack of free weights.

As all the cardio equipment faced the far wall where rows of TVs hung, Jordan could only see the backs of the people sweating away. Most were women in tight leggings though a few men dotted the landscape as well. A blond woman near the back caught Jordan's eye, and while she couldn't be sure until she got closer, she was almost positive that it was Krissy.

Swallowing her trepidation, she squared her shoulders and stepped in that direction. A few steps more revealed it was indeed the woman she sought. Krissy's cadence had slowed on the elliptical. Another few steps and Jordan discerned the reason. Her cell phone was in her hand, and somehow Jordan just knew that "he" was on the other end.

"Hi Krissy," Jordan said coming equal to the machine.

Krissy's face flamed a subtle shade of pink, and she furtively clicked a few buttons before dropping the phone into the cup holder of the machine. "Hi Jordan. I was just... checking with the babysitter."

"No, you weren't." Jordan stepped onto the neighboring machine, "but that's why I'm here today. I need to talk to you about Phil."

Krissy's eyes shifted to the right and her forehead wrinkled. "Phil? I don't know a Phil." Her protests were cut short by the chiming of her phone notification and the subtle pink shifted to a scarlet color.

"You're in danger, Krissy." Jordan allowed the words to come from a place other than her head. "James is close to discovering your secret, and while you will end up with custody of the kids, they will hate you for years to come because of this."

"How do you know about James or my kids?" Krissy's eyes darted left and right as if seeking a hidden camera or a spy feeding Jordan words.

"Do you want to go somewhere we can talk more privately?" The last thing Jordan wanted was Krissy making a scene in the middle of the gym and getting them both kicked out.

THE STILL SMALL VOICE | 53

"No!" Krissy's loud voice caused a few people nearby to turn their direction, and she lowered it for the next few words. "I want to know how you know about my family."

Jordan took a deep breath and then stared at Krissy. "I know this will sound crazy, but I was shown your face and circumstances in a vision from God. He wants me to tell you to give up Phil, to come home, and that if you don't, you will lose your family."

"That's ridiculous. God doesn't talk to anyone that way anymore." Krissy turned her face away and pumped the arm bars on the machine to match the quickened pace of her feet.

"He does if people will listen. Maybe not as clear as I get, but that still small voice that whispers something isn't right or that guilty feeling that causes you to hide your phone or lie about who you were talking to are all God's way of trying to speak to you."

Krissy's feet slowed, and her face turned to Jordan. Wide eyes informed Jordan she had hit a nerve, and the tone of Krissy's voice held a note of acceptance tinged with desperation. "But Phil makes me happy. I don't love James anymore, and surely God would want me to be happy."

Jordan shook her head. "You know that isn't right. God wants you to be holy, and if you really stop and think about it, you will understand all those signs have been his way of telling you that what you are doing isn't right."

Krissy opened her mouth to protest, but then shut it again. Her blue eyes shifted back and forth as if debating within herself. Jordan waited, knowing there wasn't much else she could say to change the woman's mind at this point.

"Is... is it too late?" Krissy asked, her voice barely more than a whisper.

Jordan smiled and shook her head. "It's never too late to come home to God. No matter what you've done, He is waiting with open arms."

at arrived at work early the next morning to make up for arriving late and leaving early the day before. She was dismayed to see the temp behind the reception desk once again. What was going on with the other woman? Was she sick? Had she quit?

When Kat reached her office, she dropped her bag and turned on the computer. Her in-box had quite a few messages, and she began scanning them pausing when she saw scan results for Cade. Her heart froze. Would it be good news? She clicked on the email and her jaw dropped. The scan showed no tumor? How was that even possible? She needed to order another scan right away.

Pushing back her chair, she strode purposefully out of her office and right into a solid chest.

"Whoa, where are you off to in such a hurry?"

Dr. Gibson. She should have known. He seemed to be everywhere she was lately. Did he ever work? "I wanted to talk to the radiologist and order some more scans."

"Good news?" His right brow rose on his forehead and he had this look like he knew something she didn't.

"Maybe, but really strange. My patient's tumor is gone. Or at least that's what the report says. It seems too good to be true."

"Well, I'll be. Is this the one I've been praying for?"

She narrowed her eyes at him. Did he really think his prayer had saved this child? "Yes, it is."

His lips broke into a wide smile. "Then I doubt the report is wrong." He leaned closer to her and lowered his voice to a whisper. "I told you God still worked miracles."

"Yeah, maybe. Or maybe the scan is just wrong. Either way I want a second scan."

He shrugged. "Suit yourself, but my bet is it will be a waste. I think God may be trying to get your attention."

Her attention? What on earth would He want her attention for? She hadn't been very faithful recently. She hadn't even prayed for Cade though she had kept saying she would. Kat shook her head to clear her thoughts and realized Dr. Gibson was walking away. "Hey, do you know what happened to our receptionist?"

He turned back to her and tilted his head. "Didn't you hear? She quit. Said she felt like she didn't matter here. I guess no one ever thanked her for all she did." He held her gaze a moment longer and then continued down the hallway.

A feeling of guilt sprouted in Kat's stomach. She should have thanked the woman, but she'd been too focused on her own life as usual.

"I'm sorry, were you talking to me, Dr. Jameson?"

Kat turned to see the young temp behind her, a bewildered expression on her face. "No, I was talking to..." She looked back but Dr. Gibson was gone. "Never mind." With a sigh and a promise to do better, Kat continued her trek to the radiologist.

She knocked gently on his door jamb when she arrived.

He looked up and motioned her in. "What can I do for, Dr. Jameson?"

Kat bit her bottom lip and stepped inside. "It's about Cade's scans. I don't mean to question your judgment, but is there any possibility you read them wrong?"

Lines of confusion sprouted on his forehead and he leaned back in his chair and crossed his arms. "Let me get this straight? I give you the great news that your patient is in remission and instead of being happy, you think I messed up?"

Kat took a deep breath. That hadn't come out the way she wanted. "I'm sorry. It's just that the tumor wasn't shrinking at all, and now it's just gone? I simply find it hard to believe. Can we just do another scan? To be sure?"

"There's no need to do another scan, but if you feel that strongly about it, then order it. I'll look over it again, but just so you know, his insurance may not cover it. Two scans that closely might raise flags."

"I'll cover the cost if necessary. I just want to be sure. No reason to give a child false hope if it was just a mistake. And thank you." Kat hurried back to her office before he could change his mind and quickly filled out an order to perform another scan. She only hoped Cade's mother wouldn't ask why; she didn't want to have to tell the woman she didn't believe her son had been miraculously healed.

And, of course, that led to a bigger question of why didn't Kat believe Cade could be miraculously healed. Didn't she believe Jesus could still perform miracles? The truth was, she'd never seen a miracle occur until now. She'd always claimed to have faith she believed it could happen, but now when faced with the possibility it had, she couldn't actually believe it. Did she have faith at all?

Kat's work kept her busy until after five that night, but when she was finally finished, she decided to hit the gym anyway. Jason had said they had classes every night until eight. Her day hadn't been bad - it was never bad when a patient went into remission - but she still felt the need to pound out some of the confusion still rattling around in her head.

"Back for more torture?" Jason asked, pointing his

half-eaten granola bar at Kat as she neared the desk on the way into class. His bare feet, propped once again on top, made her wonder if he even owned shoes. Shaking her head, she smiled at the air of confidence he exuded and wished she could be a little more like that.

She shrugged. "What can I say? I'm a sadist."

"Hah, I think we all are here," he said.

Kat was about to reply when her phone buzzed. Pulling it out, she flicked the screen to see a message from Stella.

Join me for dinner tonight?

Kat's brow furrowed. Stella usually had dinner on the table by six so that she could get Maddie bathed and into bed by eight. Why were they eating so late?

"Boyfriend?" Jason asked, sliding his feet off the desk and leaning forward without making a sound. Kat glanced at him. Was that a hint of jealousy lacing his voice?

Kat shook her head. "No, friend. There is no boyfriend." She tapped out a quick response to Stella stating she would be there around seven and shoved the phone back in her pocket.

Jason stood and suddenly Kat was sure he was about to ask her out. Not wanting to say no, but not trusting herself to say yes, she opened her mouth first. "I guess I better get changed." She continued to the dressing room without waiting for him to answer.

She wanted him to ask her out, but not right now.

Right now, there was still too much on her plate. She needed to figure her own mess out before she started dealing with someone else's mess too. Kat suddenly found herself at this weird place of wondering if she really was a believer and if not if she wanted to be.

As she entered the locker room, she tossed her bag on a bench and fished her clothes out before stepping into one of the dressing rooms. She locked the door behind her, wishing it went all the way to the floor. The foot gap at the bottom wouldn't show anyone in the outer room anything other than her feet, but it was enough of a gap that someone could put their head under the door if he or she had such a notion.

Keeping her eyes on the gap, she tugged off her shirt, replacing it with the sports bra and breathable shirt. Then she shimmied out of her jeans, replacing them with her black spandex pants. After folding her street clothes so she could shove them back in her gym bag, she opened the door.

The outer room was empty except for a girl, her brown hair in two pigtail braids, who sat with her arms crossed staring at Kat. Ice flowed from her stare. "He likes you, you know?" The girl's voice was cool.

Kat blinked and glanced around her to make sure the girl was speaking to her. "I'm sorry, who?"

"Jason."

A heat scalded across Kat's porcelain face. She hated

that she blushed so easily. Crossing to her bag, she began shoving her clothes in. "Oh, well, he seems very nice, but I... my life is complicated right now."

"He deserves better than complicated." The girl stood and pulled back her shoulders. She was shorter than Kat, but scrappy. "Don't lead him on if you aren't serious."

"I wasn't..." Kat stammered, but the girl was gone before she could finish the sentence. *What was that about?* She didn't think she had been leading Jason on; she had barely spoken to him.

With a shake of her head, she grabbed her gloves and headed out to join the class.

Jason seemed to pay extra attention to her during the hour-long workout. He was constantly coming by and commenting on her form or complimenting a move if she did something well. While she enjoyed the attention, her eyes kept darting around for the girl with the braids. Thankfully, she was much more advanced, so she was working with the other group that Brian, the owner, was leading.

When class ended, Kat gathered her things and headed for the door before Jason could come find her. She didn't want to have to say no to him, and she didn't want another run in with the girl.

She pulled into Stella's driveway a few minutes later, locked the car, and walked up the short walkway. Kat didn't bother with the bell or knocking; she just opened the front door and walked in. "Stella? I'm here."

There was no response, so Kat dropped her bag at the table by the door and continued into the kitchen. Where was everyone? Stella had invited her over and now no one was around? "Maddie? Patrick?"

Kat headed into the connected dining room and her heart stopped. Stella lay on the floor, her eyes closed. Kat rushed to her side, pulling her phone out of her pocket as she did. As one hand frantically felt for a pulse, the other dialed 911.

"911, what's your emergency?"

"This is Dr. Jameson. I'm at 7552 Wilderness Court. I have a patient who is unconscious and unresponsive, and I need an ambulance right now."

"All right, Dr. Jameson. I'm dispatching the ambulance. Is the patient breathing?"

Kat closed her eyes and took a deep breath to force herself to focus. She could do this. She was trained to do this. Yes, there was a pulse under her finger. It was weak and thready, but it was there. "Yes, the patient is breathing, but her pulse is weak."

"Thank you. ETA on the ambulance is five minutes. Please stay on the line until they arrive."

Come on, Stella. Hang in there.

THURSDAY, WASHINGTON

K at stared at the casket being lowered into the ground, numb to the chill that had descended around her. It wasn't possible. Stella couldn't be dead; hadn't they just had lunch together yesterday? No, today was Thursday evening, and they had gotten together for lunch on Sunday after church. It seemed ages ago.

Though Kat had found Stella alive Tuesday night, she'd died on the operating table. A ruptured cerebral aneurysm was the official diagnosis which explained her headaches. However, the explanation did nothing to fill the hole in Kat's heart.

A tug on her hand snapped her eyes open and drew her attention away from the casket for a moment. Maddie's strawberry blond hair and sad blue eyes looked up at her. "Aunt Kat, when is mommy coming back? I miss her."

As the tears fell freely down Maddie's angelic face, Kat's own tears welled up behind her eyes. Blinking to keep them at bay as long as possible, she lowered herself to Maddie's height. She placed her hands on the girl's shoulders and stared into her eyes. Though only five, Maddie was precocious and always insisted people talk to her like an adult. She didn't like sugar coating, and she could always tell when someone wasn't giving her the full story. The hushed conversation of the other mourners turned into a soft hum as Kat focused her full attention on the small child.

"I'm so sorry angel, but mommy isn't coming back. She's up in Heaven with God, but we'll see her when we get there." Kat's voice broke as she finished the statement, and she had to turn her head to hide the tears that had slipped out.

"But why would God take my mommy? Doesn't He know that I need her more?" The angst in the voice pulled at Kat's heart and hammered home just how young Maddie really was.

Kat could only shake her head. Emotion constricted her throat, cutting off the ability to whisper words that wouldn't console Maddie anyway. She pulled Maddie in for a fierce hug, her eyes seeking Patrick over Maddie's shoulder. As their gazes locked, the silent message that passed between them needed no audible sound. How Maddie was going to survive this was the mantra on both of their minds.

"Come on, Maddie, let's go home." Patrick stepped forward and touched her shoulder. The little girl turned her liquid pools on Kat.

"Go ahead honey. I'll come by soon." Kat managed to whisper though the words burned in her throat. She gave Maddie a final hug and watched the two walk away. Regardless of her own feelings, it was a promise she intended to keep. That little girl would need a woman in her life, and Kat was determined she wouldn't let her down.

As the rest of the crowd thinned out, Kat decided to go home too, though she worried she was still too emotional to be driving. She looked at the fire and ice rose in her hand—Stella's favorite—and thought back to the first time Stella had mentioned them. They had been twenty, enjoying college, and worried about boys, which was why they were taking the quiz in the first place.

"Okay, favorite type of flower," Kat asked, reading the question aloud from the magazine.

Stella smiled. "Fire and ice roses."

Kat rolled her eyes and shook her head. "No, come on, Stella, something easy that someone could match to. Otherwise you ruin the quiz."

Stella crossed her arms and pursed her lips. "Well, you asked, and those are my favorite."

"Why? I mean I know they're pretty but why do you have to be so difficult?"

"They remind me of us. You're the fire, and I'm the ice."

Kat stared at her. While it was true that she was the spontaneous, impetuous one, she certainly didn't consider Stella to be cold. Stella was quieter and more reserved, but she was one of the kindest people Kat knew. "Why are you the ice?"

"Well, I can't be the fire," Stella smiled, but a sadness remained in her eyes. "Sometimes I feel as if you'll go off to take on the world, and I'll be all alone, like the ice."

Coincidentally, it had been just a month later that she met Patrick and Kat had felt more like the ice, but she hadn't minded because Stella had been right. Kat had plans to take on the world, and she wouldn't have done it if Stella had been alone. When she married Patrick though, it allowed Kat to focus on med school. Four years away had been long enough though, and when a resident position opened back in Washington, Kat had been ready to return home.

"Goodbye my friend," Kat whispered as the memory faded. She kissed the rose and let it fall onto the casket. Then she walked out of the shelter of the pop-up tent into the cold, drizzling rain that created a gray and dreary landscape, much like her feelings inside. The rain pelted her head, molding her dark hair to her face, but Kat didn't care. Nor did the biting cold affect her.

As she drove back to her house, her thoughts were everywhere and nowhere at the same time. She pulled into her driveway and parked the car, locking it without thinking. Her feet carried her up her front walk and, on autopilot, her hands found the right key and opened the door.

Kat didn't bother to turn the lights on as she entered the front door. The darkness suited her mood. After locking the door behind her, she ambled down the beige carpeted hallway and into her bedroom. It was a path she knew by heart and one she didn't need lights to travel. Her room was also dark though a faint light crept in through the window. Crossing to the window, Kat pulled back the magenta curtain and turned her face to the Heavens.

How could a loving God do that? The words whispered in her head.

"Why God? Why her? Stella was a good person. She followed you. She had a child!" The last word came out as a sob. Why did God allow bad things to happen to good people, to his followers even? Why would he save Cade but take Stella's life?

Anger fueled inside her, edging out the sadness. Her hands shook at her sides, and the urge to hit something, to throw something welled up within. She turned from the window, seeking the object she wanted to throw most. Her eyes landed on it, laying nonchalantly on the nightstand next to her bed.

Her jaw clenched, and she stomped over to the small brown table and picked up her black leather Bible. A trembling traveled up her arms, and her knuckles turned white. "I hate you God." Seething, she drew her arm back. The bible flew out like a missile, hitting the far wall and falling to the floor on its spine, but instead of closing, the book opened, its pages staring up at the ceiling.

The words called out to her, but Kat folded in on herself and collapsed to the floor on the opposite side of the room. Her hands covered her face as the tears she had been fighting finally won and spilled over her cheeks, starting as trickles but soon coming down in great gushes accompanied with hitching sobs.

"I don't understand why you took her God. Please help me understand." Kat repeated the words over and over as she rocked back and forth, desperately hoping for some clue, some guidance from a God she had always associated with love.

~

Afriel turned questioning eyes on Galadriel. "I don't understand either. Won't this push her away?"

"Sometimes it does, but it can often bring people

closer. We are not always informed of God's plan, but we must keep doing our jobs. I do fear she will be under attack more now as she will be more vulnerable. We will have to stand vigilant to keep the demons at bay."

"Is it always like this?"

Galadriel smiled. "There is a spiritual war going on always until Jesus returns and sets up the new kingdom. Humans can't always see it, but yes, our job is to fight the demons they can't see. To save as many as we can."

Afriel nodded. "I will be ready then."

FRIDAY, TEXAS

ordan sat up in bed and looked around the room. The dream seemed so real, but who was the dark-haired girl with the emerald eyes? Rising from the bed, Jordan kneeled on the beige, carpeted floor and clasped her hands. She closed her eyes and cleared her mind. "Lord, I know that vision was from you, but who is she and what do I need to do?"

Jordan was becoming accustomed to the visions. They had been coming for a week now. But this time it was different. This time all she saw was the dark-haired woman staring out a window as the rain poured down. An intense sadness resided in her eyes, but her stiff posture held a note of anger or defiance. Jordan had no idea who the woman was or even where she lived. The only clue was the drizzling rain, but that could be many places.

There had also been no feeling of what she was to do next, but she was sure God would reveal it in time.

As she prayed, the small voice spoke in her head. "Do you trust Me?"

"Of course, I trust you, God." When she had first begun praying, Jordan felt self-conscious speaking aloud, even though she lived alone. Now, she felt as though God were in the room with her when she spoke.

"Do you really trust Me?" Jordan thought she had trusted him, but as the vision of what He wanted her to do filled her head, she realized the other tests were small in comparison. Why would He ask her to travel across the country?

She tried to argue with the vision. "My life is here, Lord. How will I pay my bills if I go? How will I finish college?"

"I will provide." The Lord provided an answer for each point she raised. Beaten, she accepted the vision and opened her eyes.

A year ago, she would have laughed at anyone who told her they talked to God. She'd had no time for God in her life, but when she'd been drugged and date-raped by a boy she trusted, her world turned upside down. The encounter with Amanda opened her eyes, and after giving up her baby, she turned to God for comfort. Though a loving couple adopted her son, it hadn't been easy and God had been the solace every night as she cried herself to sleep. So, she promised to do His will in her life from now on. She just hadn't been expecting Him to ask so much so soon.

Rising from her knees, she gathered up her clothes and walked down the hall to the bathroom to shower. She would need to be professional for what she needed to do if there was a hope of coming back.

～

*J*ordan pulled into the parking lot of the small pregnancy counseling center where she worked and parked the car. The way they helped her when she was seeking options impressed her so much that she jumped at the opportunity to work for them when it arose. Now she could help mothers with unplanned pregnancies the same way they had helped her. She knew the organization was a Christian one, but she would still miss a lot of work, and she had no idea if they would agree to it.

Her boss, Grace, sat in her office working on some paperwork. Jordan paused to gather her courage before knocking on the jamb. "Grace, can I have a moment of your time?"

The woman beamed at her. "Of course, Jordan, you know my door's always open. Come on in."

Jordan shuffled into the office and sat down in one of

the two empty chairs. She folded her hands in her lap and cleared her throat. "I have no idea if this is possible, but I wanted to see if I could take some time off."

Grace's large brown eyes stared evenly back at her. "Are you not happy here?"

"Oh, no, it's not that. In fact, I'm hoping maybe there's a similar center I can continue to work at. I ...um...need to go to Washington state for a time."

Grace folded her hands together and leaned back in her chair. "I see, and how long is 'a time?'"

Jordan licked her lips and shook her head. "I don't really know. I'm not even exactly sure where I'm going or what I'll be doing." She paused as she tried to think of how to present her issue to Grace. She decided straight forward would be the best way. "Are you a Christian, Grace?"

"I am."

Relief filled Jordan. That would make her next words a little easier. "Well, so am I, and lately, though I don't know why, God has been talking to me. He sends me images of people and what to say to them. I don't know who this girl is or why she's important, but this morning He told me I needed to go to Washington." Jordan bit the inside of her lip, hoping she hadn't misinterpreted God's words this morning, as she watched Grace process the information.

Grace unfolded her long, slender hands and placed her

palms together. Her chin rested on her fingertips as she regarded Jordan as if looking for any hint of deception. "I am friends with the woman who runs a similar agency out in Olympia Washington, and if God is calling you to do this, then He must have a reason. I'm not one to stand in his way. I'll call my friend Donna up there to see if she has a spot for you. I'll also hold your position, but only for the summer. If God needs you longer than that, I'll have to fill the spot with a permanent replacement."

Jordan considered this more than fair and readily agreed. After shaking hands with her boss, she left the office to return home and arrange a new living situation. Maybe she could sublet her apartment while she was gone, and she would have to find a place there fully furnished. She didn't want to haul everything she owned to Washington state only to bring it back to Texas a few months later.

Kat woke the next morning, stiff as a board. She was still in yesterday's clothes, wrinkled from their time on the floor. How she had even slept that way was beyond her, but the grief probably had something to do with it.

She stood, stretching to loosen the stiff joints and froze. A snippet of a dream resurfaced, but she couldn't remember much. Just light. A bright yellow light. Kat shook her head to dislodge the image. Why on earth would she be dreaming about lights?

Dismissing it as nothing more than her grief-stricken, overworked mind, Kat forced herself out of bed and into the shower. The warm water, which normally woke her up, now felt like tiny pellets hitting her skin.

When the shower was finished, Kat grabbed pants and

a shirt from the closet, hoping they matched but not caring enough to check. She ran a quick brush through her long, tangled hair and brushed her teeth. Then she stumbled down the hallway to the kitchen.

Just the thought of seeing patients seemed daunting today, but Kat made herself fill the coffee pot and set it percolating. Her stomach was empty, but she felt no desire for food. She wondered if she ever would again.

When the dripping slowed to a stop, Kat filled her travel mug, added her cream, turned off the pot, and gathered her things. As she walked to her car, a sick feeling sprouted in her stomach. Today would be her first day back at the hospital since Monday evening when she rode in the ambulance with Stella. Would she be able to walk into the grey building that once was her sanctuary and now held the memory of Stella's lifeless body?

Kat parked the car in her usual spot and took a deep breath. If she could just make it to the elevator, she thought she might be okay.

The hospital doors whooshed open, and the room began to press in on Kat. She'd heard the same sound Monday evening as the EMTs rushed Stella inside. Ducking her head, she hurried to the elevator and pressed the button. *Come on. Come on.*

There was a glorious ding and the doors opened. Kat punched the button for the oncology floor and sighed in relief when the doors shut. Surely this would get easier. It had to get easier.

When the doors opened on her floor, Kat averted her eyes, hoping to avoid any questions, as she made her way to the office. Another wave of relief hit her as she sank into her chair, but it was short lived.

"I heard about your friend. I'm sorry."

Kat closed her eyes. Of course, it would have to be Dr. Gibson. He must work as much as she did to be in on a Saturday again, and yet, she had no idea what he did here. Somehow, he seemed to know everything and want to be involved in all of it. "Thank you."

"How are you doing?"

Kat rubbed a hand across her forehead. "I'm okay, I guess. As good as can be expected, considering."

"Look, I'm not sure what I can do, but if I can help in any way, just let me know. I'm here for you. Whatever you need. Even if you ever just want to talk."

Kat's eyes snapped open as anger flared within her. "You want to talk? Fine, let's talk about why God saved Cade and not Stella. Huh? Why would He do that? Why would He leave a little five-year-old girl to grow up without a mother?"

A sadness filled Dr. Gibson's eyes. "God has a plan that we don't always see or understand, but I hope you're listening, Kat, because I think He's trying to get your attention."

"My attention? By killing my best friend? Well, He's got it, but I don't think it's the kind of attention He was looking for. Now, if you'll excuse me, I have two days of work to catch up on."

Dr. Gibson stared at her for another moment before exiting her office. With a sigh, Kat turned her laptop on and prepared to check the onslaught of messages. She stared at the screen, but the words made no sense. Perhaps she should have taken a few more days off. She certainly had plenty of time off stored up, but she hoped that work would provide a distraction.

Her phone chimed, and she snapped it up. She didn't even care who was on the other end as long as it distracted and filled her head for a moment. The notification showed a text from Patrick.

"Can you come to dinner tonight? Maddie has been asking for you?"

Her finger hovered over the keyboard. She wanted to see Maddie, to be there for her, but dinner at Stella's house without Stella created a feeling of dread in her stomach. Still, she had promised. Mustering her courage, she tapped out a yes and hit send.

Placing the phone back on her desk, she turned back to the computer. She was determined to do something today even if it was simply reading email.

*a*s Kat pulled up in front of the familiar house that evening, she fought the urge to reverse the car and drive away. What had she been thinking agreeing to this? It was too soon. Instead, she forced herself to put the car in park and turn off the engine.

This would be the first time she'd be in her best friend's house since the funeral. She'd been in briefly before the funeral to help Patrick pick out clothes for Stella to wear, but she'd bolted as soon as the deed was done. The thought of stepping in the house with Stella gone sent waves of nausea running through her body, but a promise was a promise and she had promised that little girl to be there for her. Though she wasn't sure how much help she would be.

Kat herself was a mess. Dark circles still ringed her normally bright green eyes, and she wasn't sure she had brushed her hair or her teeth this morning. Worse yet, she didn't care.

Deciding it didn't matter as she wasn't trying to impress Patrick and he was probably in just as rough of shape as she was, she exited the car and walked to the front door. Once there, she paused. When Stella was alive, she would walk right in, but now that she was gone, Kat had no idea if that were still acceptable. After all, she and Patrick were never that close. He was simply the man her best friend loved, but Kat had never taken the time to get to know him. The sound of the doorbell caused her to jump as she hadn't even realized she had pressed the button.

Patrick looked equally confused when he opened the door a moment later. "Oh, I thought you'd just come in." His blue eyes held none of their usual brightness, and the sprinkling of red stubble on his face told Kat he hadn't exerted the effort to shave this morning.

"I wasn't sure." She gripped the strap of her purse tighter in her hand. "It feels... different now."

Patrick nodded, but stepped back and opened the door wide enough for her to enter. "Maddie's in her room, but I have to get the spaghetti ready. Why don't you keep her company?"

"You cook?" Kat's forehead wrinkled in surprise. She hadn't meant for the question to slip out, but she couldn't remember a time in the last eight years that Stella had mentioned Patrick cooking.

"Not much." He sighed and shook his head. "But I can boil water."

Kat felt horrible for making him feel inadequate and vowed to come and cook a few nights a week. She wasn't much of a cook herself, but living alone for the last nine years had forced her to learn the necessities.

As Patrick headed back to the kitchen, Kat dropped her purse on the entry table out of habit and looked around. The room still looked as it had when Stella was alive. Stella picked the rose-colored paint that adorned the wall herself, and Kat, Stella, and Patrick spent an evening painting the large room and arguing over an episode of Chicago Fire.

The weight of losing Stella felt heavier here. Kat wondered how Maddie and Patrick could stay in this house where every room held Stella's touch. Though not a professional interior designer, Stella studied it some in college and tried out several techniques when she and Patrick bought the house. The result was a clash of country and modern that wouldn't have worked anywhere else, but seemed to work in Stella's home.

Kat continued through the living room to the hallway that led to the bedrooms. Maddie's room, decorated in Frozen theme, was on the right across from the hall bathroom. A poster of Elsa hung on the not-quite-closed door.

Kat pushed the door open a little further, tapping softly on it as she did so as not to scare Maddie who lay on her bed reading a book. At the sound of the knocking, Maddie lowered her book, and her eyes lit up.

"Aunt Kat." Maddie slammed the book shut and bounded off the bed, crossing the room in three giant strides to envelope Kat in a hug.

"Hey, Monkey," Kat replied. The nickname was given to Maddie at two when she began climbing all the furniture. Stella was terrified of her daredevil streak and rightly so because at three, she fell off the top of the bookshelf and broke her arm. The cast barely slowed her down though it had been enough to keep her from climbing the bookshelf again. "How are you doing?"

The light dimmed from Maddie's face, and her shoulders sagged. "I miss my mom."

"Me too, Maddie, me too, but your daddy is making spaghetti, your favorite." Kat changed the subject, hoping it would lighten the mood.

"He burned the toast this morning and forgot to make my lunch," Maddie said.

Though trivial in the grand scheme of things, Kat could tell this was a big deal to Maddie. "We'll have to give him some time. He's working on it." Kat tucked a stray hair behind the girl's ear. "In the meantime, how about if I come by a few nights a week and make dinner, would you like that?"

Maddie nodded and wrapped her arms around Kat's neck again.

"What were you reading?" Kat asked when it became obvious Maddie had no intention of letting go. She didn't mind hugs, but this one was stirring up emotions she didn't want to be feeling right now.

"Oh, a princess book," Maddie squealed, releasing Kat and running back to the bed to retrieve it. "My teacher just got it in, and she let me check it out first." Her chest puffed out with pride.

Kat was just about to ask her more about the book when Patrick's voice carried down the hall that dinner was ready. "Well, I guess we better go eat. You can tell me more about it after dinner."

Maddie stuck out her bottom lip in a small pout but put the book back on her bed and followed Kat out of the room.

Patrick had set the small kitchen table, but he had set a plate down in front of Stella's usual chair. Kat couldn't bring herself to take that seat, so she moved the plate to her regular place while Patrick's back was turned. If he noticed when he returned with the spaghetti, he was polite enough not to say anything.

He dished up spaghetti on each of their plates before sitting in his own chair and reaching for Maddie's and Kat's hands. Kat let him take her hand though she was surprised he was still praying to God. Wasn't he as angry as she was?

Patrick and Maddie both closed their eyes, but Kat left hers open even though it felt very unnatural. She hadn't been great at praying before Stella died on Monday. And she hadn't prayed since, but that was not a dinner conversation. Kat played along and kept silent. She did *not*, however, echo the amen at the end.

The spaghetti was not the best, but Patrick managed not to screw it up too badly. She only found a few noodles still clumped together as she ate. He'd even thrown a salad together, though Kat presumed it came from of a bag. Still, at least she knew Maddie wouldn't starve.

Patrick and Kat took turns talking about their respective days, then they both asked questions of Maddie to find out about her school day. The conversation was stiff and formulaic, but Kat hoped it would become easier the more time she spent here and the more she got to know Patrick as someone other than Stella's guy.

When dinner ended, she helped him clear the table while Maddie played in the other room. Then they joined Maddie in the living room and watched Frozen for probably the hundredth time since the movie had come out. Maddie sang along with every song and even spoke some of the lines with the characters. Kat shot Patrick a look over Maddie's head, but he merely shrugged and turned back to the TV.

Before the movie hit the halfway mark, Maddie yawned and leaned against Patrick. He scooped her up and carried her down the hall. Kat followed behind, wanting a glimpse of Patrick in action. It wasn't that she thought he couldn't do it; she was sure he had at some point in the last eight years, but she was curious how different his routine was from Stella's.

He laid Maddie in the bed and turned to the dresser to grab pajamas. Kat leaned against the door frame, wanting to be unobtrusive but still involved. As Patrick changed

Maddie into her pajamas, she roused slightly and smiled up at him.

"All right monkey. Let's pray," Patrick said.

At the mention of those words, a stone settled in Kat's stomach and she left the room. She didn't need to hear any more praying right now.

She wandered back into the living room and stood there undecided. Now that Maddie was asleep, should she go? Would it be weird if she stayed? So much was different now and she found the waters hard to navigate.

"Lost in thought?"

She jumped at Patrick's voice behind her, then turned to face him. "I was debating whether to stay or leave. Normally, Stella and I would have gone off to chat while you did whatever you do, but now,"—she shrugged— "I wasn't sure."

"Look, I know it's hard and new, but maybe it would help if we clarified a few things." Patrick walked past her and into the kitchen.

Kat couldn't argue with that and she followed his footsteps. He opened the fridge and pulled out a beer, offering her one, but Kat shook her head. The taste of beer had never grown on her. She sat on a barstool, and he leaned against the counter across from her.

"How about this? You can still come and go without ringing the bell. You have a key, right?"

Kat nodded. Stella had given her a copy years ago

when she offered to watch Maddie while Stella and Patrick had their date night.

"Okay, feel free to use it. I want you to help Maddie whenever she needs it or you feel like you need it. If you want to stay after she goes to sleep, you're welcome to. If not, just lock the door behind you, so I know, how's that?"

It felt like a business arrangement, but one that Kat could agree to. "Sounds like a plan. I guess I'll be going now, but I promised Maddie I'd come a few times a week to cook dinner."

Patrick shot her a look full of gratitude. "Thanks, I think we'll grow tired of spaghetti and mac n cheese pretty quickly, and that's about all that's in my repertoire right now."

Kat heard the sadness in his voice, but she had no words of comfort. "I'll come tomorrow. Have a good night." She pushed herself off the barstool, grabbed her purse off the entry table, and headed outside.

As the outside air hit her, the grief she had been holding back flooded forward. Tears spilled down her cheeks, and the anger that had remained checked all evening flared again. Her face turned heavenward and she raised her fist to shake it at God. "I don't know why he still prays to you, but I'm done. A loving God wouldn't do what you did."

She paused, expecting a flash of lightning or some other visual display of God's anger, but the sky remained silent. "Are you even listening? Do you even care about us?" Nothing but silence and a few stares from the few other people on the street came back to Kat. Disgusted, she lowered her fists, got in her car, and drove home.

~

Galadriel scowled as the demons sped away from Kat. He wasn't allowed to fight them. Not yet, but seeing them whisper in her ear had almost been more than he could bear.

"What do we do now?" Afriel asked. "Do we go after them?" He pulled his sword from the scabbard and took up a fighting stance.

"No, our job is not them. Not yet. We stay with Kat. We encourage her. But don't worry, their time is coming."

SATURDAY, WASHINGTON

*K*at sat upright in bed, immediately seeking the time on her alarm clock. Had she overslept? Was that what had woken her so? The red numbers read 5:20. It was not yet morning and definitely not time for her alarm, so what had woken her?

She lay back on her pillow and closed her eyes, trying to focus. Something about lights, but she couldn't place what. Annoyed, Kat tried to go back to sleep, but her mind would not stop churning. Frustrated, she decided to just get up and put on a pot of coffee.

As the coffee percolated, Kat flicked on the news. A house fire had killed three; an elderly man was beaten and robbed; and a bus driver was under investigation for an inappropriate relationship with a student. Disgusted, Kat clicked the channel to a game show, remembering why she didn't watch the news.

"Do you care about any of us? You could stop this, you know?" The deafening silence answered her. Had she been wrong all these years to believe God was listening?

The coffee stopped dripping, and Kat returned to the kitchen to pour herself a cup. When that cup was empty, she dressed and headed off to work. There were no patients to see today, but she still had a lot of work to catch up on after missing most of the previous week. Kat's only hope was that Dr. Gibson wouldn't be there. She didn't need another person telling her to trust God or pray about her anger.

Her luck held and by five pm, though Kat had consumed another three cups of coffee she still felt as if she could go home, fall into bed, and sleep for a week. Her sleep had been anything but peaceful since Stella's death, and she wasn't sure how much longer she could keep up the way she was going.

After shutting down her computer and gathering her purse and water, Kat headed to her car. She needed to stop at the grocery store before going to Maddie's house. Street tacos were on the menu for tonight, and she still needed some ingredients.

She pulled into the local Albertsons and hastened into the store. Meat, tortillas, cheese, cilantro, peppers–she rattled the list off in her head as she scooped up the ingredients, dropping them in the basket slung over her left arm.

As she made her way to the check-out lane, she cursed her forgetfulness. She hadn't brought in her tote bag. Again. She hated this mandated 'no plastic bag' rule because she often forgot her bags at home or in the car, and she hated having to pay for paper bags, especially since they either took up space on her bar or in her trash when she got home. Worse, she knew there was a bag in her car today. It would be laughing at her from the passenger seat as soon as she got to her car.

"Would you like a bag?" the checker asked.

"No." Kat scowled at the young woman. "I'll just carry it out."

The checker's eyebrows rose, but she said nothing, just smiled and scanned the items. "That will be $24.10 today." Kat pulled out her debit card and swiped it in the reader.

After inputting her pin and tucking the receipt from the checker in her pocket, she stacked the items in her arms. When she felt they were as secure as they would get, she ventured back out to the car.

With each step, her load shifted minutely and just before she reached the car, the cheese slipped from her grip landing on the pavement. Thankfully, the bag that held it did not burst; her cheese remained intact. Still it was enough to fire up her new hair-trigger temper.

"Argh." Kat tried to shift the remaining load in her hands to free one up to snatch the cheese back.

After a few unsuccessful tries, she scooted the cheese with her foot the remaining few feet to the car. She put a few of the groceries on the hood of the car to free her right hand. Then she fished in her purse for the keys, hitting the unlock button on the key fob. Sure enough, the green cloth bag mocked her from the front passenger seat.

Kat snatched it open and crammed the ingredients still cradled in her arm in. Then she grabbed the ones off the hood and the cheese off the ground and stuffed them in as well. She wasn't even sure why she was so angry, but she couldn't seem to abate it either. Ever since Stella's death, her temper flared much faster and burned brighter.

A few calming breaths seemed to tamp it down slightly, enough that Kat felt okay driving, and a few minutes later she pulled up to Stella's house. It was weird that she still called it Stella's house when Stella had been gone nearly a week, but it was a hard habit to break. Patrick's car wasn't in the driveway, so Kat kept her keys out as she walked up to the front door. The bag of ingredients pulled heavily on her right side, throwing her a little off balance.

After trying the door and finding it locked, she flipped through her keys until she found the right one and let herself inside. She crossed the entry way and opened her mouth to holler for Stella–her usual greeting–before the stillness of the house hit her. Stella wasn't here. Stella would never be here again.

Kat slammed the door behind her and locked it. The small wooden sign 'As for me and my house, we serve the Lord' that hung above the door banged against the wall from the impact. Fighting the anger, Kat leaned back against the door and closed her eyes, taking a few, deep breaths. When the red faded from her vision, she continued into the kitchen and pulled out the ingredients.

Kat had just started cutting the vegetables when she heard the garage door open and the sound of running feet.

"Aunt Kat," Maddie said as she burst into the kitchen and hugged Kat's legs.

"Hey, monkey." Kat leaned down to give Maddie a hug before standing to continue chopping the vegetables.

"What are we having?" Maddie stretched on her tiptoes to see the top of the bar.

"Street tacos with extra cheese."

"Mm, I love cheese." Maddie smiled and rubbed her belly.

Kat smiled down at Maddie glad she could still find joy even with her life turned upside down. She wished she could do the same. Patrick entered the kitchen then and tossed his briefcase on the other side of the bar.

"Hi." Even the simple word felt weird coming out of her mouth as she stood in her best friend's kitchen, greeting her daughter and husband like they were her own.

He must have felt the same way because he raised his hand in an awkward wave before continuing down the hallway. Maddie filled Kat in on her day at school, which at least kept her mind busy, but the feeling that she was playing house in someone else's life wouldn't go away.

The trio sat down for dinner when the food was ready, and once again, Kat refused to join the prayer. If Patrick noticed, he said nothing, just thanked her for the food before piling the meat and vegetables on his tortilla.

When dinner was finished, Kat collected the dishes and rinsed them in the sink. Patrick and Maddie were in the living room, and she could hear their voices as they laughed over a game of Candyland. As the water glided over the plate in her hand, sweeping the left-over bits of food off, Kat wondered if there was something wrong with her. Why did they seem okay while she was such a wreck?

"She'd like to say goodnight to you."

Kat jumped at the voice, not realizing she had lost track of time as her mind wandered. She shut off the water and loaded the plate clutched in her hand in the dishwasher.

"Sorry, I didn't mean to scare you."

"No, it's fine. I didn't know how late it had gotten. Of course, I'll go say goodnight." She left Patrick in the kitchen as she walked down the hall to Maddie's room.

Kat pushed the door open and stuck her head inside. "Maddie?"

"Aunt Kat, will you pray with me?" Maddie's voice was heavy with sleep.

Kat paused. She had no desire to pray, but how could she explain that to Maddie? "How about you pray for both of us?"

Maddie nodded and mumbled a sleepy prayer, thanking God for the day and asking him to look after her mother. Kat choked back tears and kissed Maddie's forehead before returning to the living room where Patrick was standing, flipping channels on the remote.

"How can you still pray with her?" Kat asked. A mixture of venom and sadness laced her voice.

"Why wouldn't I?" His brows knitted together, but his attention was still on the TV. Another few clicks landed him on the news and he tossed the remote on the couch. Then he turned, ignoring her glaring eyes and crossed arms, and walked past her into the kitchen.

Miffed, she followed him, watching him open the refrigerator and pull out a beer. "Because God took Stella."

"He didn't take her," Patrick said, shaking his head. "She had an aneurysm that burst. You want one?" He held the beer out to her.

Rolling her eyes, she shook her head. "No, you know I don't drink beer. Well, didn't protect her then. Why didn't

He give the first doctor the knowledge to catch it? Or why didn't He allow her to see a specialist sooner? She had an appointment booked for later that week, for goodness' sake. How can you still pray to a loving God who didn't protect her? Maddie asked God to look after her mother in there. She shouldn't have to do that." The anger was fueling again and Kat's voice had taken on an unnatural edge.

He tipped back the beer, ignoring her question. She watched his Adam's apple bob up and down as he downed most of the beer. "You're right." He set the beer down and turned his hazel eyes on her. "She shouldn't have to ask God to look after her mother, but she does. That is the hand dealt to her, and I am trying to keep life as normal as I can for her considering that fact. We prayed to God before the accident, and we will continue to pray to Him after. Sometimes praying is the only thing that gets me out of bed in the morning."

Red flashed in Kat's vision, and her hands clenched at her side. "Are you saying I don't have a right to be angry at God? You think I should still pray to Him?"

"I do think you should still pray, but you must come to that conclusion on your own. Look, I'm angry and sad too, but I can't let those emotions control my life." He opened the fridge and grabbed another beer. "I have a daughter to raise."

His words felt like a slap in her face. She wasn't

Maddie's mother, but she was here, helping. She had been here twice this week already. Her mouth dropped open, and she shook her head at him.

"I'm sorry." He took a step toward her.

"Don't be." She stepped away from him. "I'm not her mother. I get it. I'll just go."

"Kat." His voice carried after her, but she had already left the kitchen. She snatched her purse from the table and yanked the door open. She wanted to slam it again, but the thought of waking Maddie stopped her just in time. Instead, she quietly closed it behind her before stomping to her car. She didn't know where she was going, so she let herself drive aimlessly, landing in the parking lot of the same small neighborhood bar she had entered a week ago.

Could it really only be a week ago that she had been here angry that Cade had cancer? Now, he was in remission, but her best friend was dead.

Her phone buzzed as she parked the car. Patrick's apology filled the screen. She wouldn't stay mad at him for long; she knew she had overreacted. He was dealing with the same pain she was though he seemed to handle it much better. While she couldn't seem to control the anger flooding her body, at least her logic usually caught up quickly. So, she'd accept his apology, but not yet. Right now, she felt the need to drown her sorrows.

The bar was a little fuller tonight, but Kat found a free barstool.

"Hey, haven't seen you at the gym. You decide it's not for you?"

Kat looked up at Jason who was smiling down at her. "Sorry, my best friend died Monday. I've been a little preoccupied."

His eyes widened and his brows rose on his forehead. "Whoa, really? Man, I'm sorry. Here, first drink is on the house. Tequila Sunrise, right?"

Kat nodded and a moment later, a short glass with the yellow and orange liquid appeared in front of her. She downed it without hesitation and signaled Jason to fill another.

"Kat, I know it's not my place," he placed another glass in front of her, "but I don't think drinking your feelings away is healthy."

"You're right. It's not your place. Just fill my drinks. I don't need a shrink."

Jason shrugged and turned to his other patrons, and Kat sipped this drink, hating how angry she was but unsure of how to stop it.

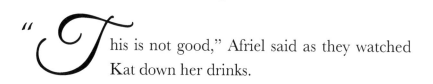

"This is not good," Afriel said as they watched Kat down her drinks.

"No, it isn't, but all is not lost yet. Remember, He has a plan."

"Does this happen often with humans?"

"Far too often," Galadriel said sadly. "Instead of relying on God the Father, they turn to other substances, other people for fulfillment. But they can never find it in those things. Only in God."

MONDAY, WASHINGTON

"*K*at, are you listening?"

Kat turned her attention from the crisp fall day to her friend. Her golden hair glistened in the sun, and her blue eyes shone brightly. They had decided to enjoy the last bit of warm weather by having a picnic lunch at a nearby park. "Sure, Stella, what did you say?"

"You need to pay attention. God needs you to listen and see."

Kat laughed. "God doesn't need me, Stella. He has you. You've always been more faithful than I have."

Stella's eyes grew serious as the sparkle left them. They changed from blue to gray. "No, Kat. It is very important that you listen. Listen to the still, small voice."

Kat sat upright in bed. Her heart hammered in her chest. First lights and now Stella. What did these dreams mean? Were they ever going to stop?

She kicked back the covers and stumbled out of bed to the bathroom. As the light came on, she cringed at the dark circles under her eyes. Her skin had taken on a sallow tone as well. If she didn't get some sleep soon, she would scare her patients.

After a shower and a granola bar, Kat headed into work, hoping today Dr. Gibson would be too busy to nag her.

She threw herself into checking up on patients and documenting charts and before she knew it, her stomach was rumbling. Kat hadn't eaten much lately, but she knew she needed to. With a sigh, she pushed back from her desk to head to the cafeteria. She had brought nothing to eat.

As she passed the receptionist's desk, her feet slowed. It was the same temp who had taken over when the other girl left. Stephanie something or other. She still looked a little frazzled, like she hadn't figured out the job yet, but it was the light surrounding her that had caught Kat's attention.

She looked up to see if the light were coming from above, but it was just the ceiling. Her head turned in a slow circle, but there was nothing in the room that would cast a light on her.

Stephanie looked up. "Did you need something, Dr. Jameson?"

"Um, no, I just wanted to let you know I was going to lunch in case anyone called. And you're doing a good job."

The last six words flew out of her mouth before she had time to think about them.

Stephanie smiled and but the light didn't fade. "Really? Thank you. I've felt like I've been letting you all down and maybe this wasn't the job for me, but I really like it here. I'm so glad you said something."

Kat nodded and returned the smile. At least she hoped it was a smile. She had no idea where those words had come from. In fact, she was almost certain she hadn't even thought them. Sleep. That had to be it. The lack of decent sleep must be catching up to her. Before Stephanie could say anything else, Kat continued to the elevator, keeping her head down so as not to make eye contact with anyone else.

The cafeteria was emptying when she arrived. Kat was glad she had come later and missed the lunch crowd. With the way she was feeling today, she just wanted to grab food, eat, and then go hide out in her office again.

Her luck held and she ate in silence. Then she threw her trash away and made it back to her office without another incident. Still the image of the light didn't leave her mind. Was it the same light from her dreams? She wished she could remember them more, but it was like reaching for a feather that the wind blew away just as your fingertips touched it.

She shook her head to clear the image and tried to focus on her work, but she found herself staring at the screen and aimlessly clicking buttons. At least until her phone rang at three. Patrick. Her heart clenched in her chest and she took a deep breath. *Please don't let it be bad news. I can't take any more.*

"Patrick? What's the matter?"

"It's Maddie. She's crying uncontrollably. Something about a graduation. I can't get her to stop. Can you come now? I need your help."

Patrick had never sounded so frantic. "Of course, I'll be right there." The line clicked, and Kat shut down her computer and grabbed her things.

"Is everything okay, Dr. Jameson?" Stephanie asked as Kat rushed past the reception desk.

"I think so, but I have to leave early tonight. Can you hold my calls? I'll be in early tomorrow."

Stephanie nodded and Kat continued to the elevator. Just before the doors closed, she saw Dr. Gibson looking her direction. She was sure he'd be at her office tomorrow with questions.

As soon as she parked the car at Patrick's house, Kat rushed inside. Maddie's loud crying pulled at her heartstrings.

Patrick sat next to Maddie on her bed. His arm was wrapped around her shoulder and his hand patted her ineffectively. He looked completely out of his element. His eyes sought hers with a silent plead for help. Kat entered the room and sat on Maddie's other side.

"Hey monkey, come here." Kat pulled Maddie into her lap. Patrick dropped his arm from Maddie's shoulders and stood. Kat nodded at his questioning eyes, and as he left the room, she turned her attention back to the sobbing child in her arms. "Can you tell me what happened?"

Maddie tried to get the words out in between the hitching sobs shaking her little body. "It was graduation day... No one was there for me... Everyone asked where my mom and dad were... They should have been there, mommy should have been there... I miss mommy." The last word came out as a three-syllable wail and the tears increased their trek down her cheeks.

"Oh, monkey." Kat squeezed the girl tight, caressing her hair and wishing she had a solution.

~

"She's finally asleep," Kat said forty-five minutes later when she returned to the living room. Patrick sat with his head in his hands. His copper hair poked in a few different directions, belaying the obvious raking it had recently suffered. "Why didn't you tell me? I could have been there."

"I didn't even know." His voice was low, his face still pointed at the floor. "Stella was always the one who took off work for events like this." He raised his head, blue eyes streaked with red. "What if I can't do this, Kat? What if I can't raise her alone?"

The anger flared inside her again. How could God do this? How could He leave Maddie with no mother? The need to hit something descended on her like a hawk, and her hands clenched at her side. "It will be okay. We'll figure out a way to make this work." She sat beside him on the couch and wrapped her arm around his shoulder. "You're not alone; you'll always have me." Her pinched voice took away some of the relief her words were meant to hold, but they seemed to satisfy him.

He looked up at her, gratitude swimming in his tear-filled eyes. Kat knew she should stay to console him, but her own emotions were sparking and she needed to get away from him, from Maddie, from the house before her own floodgates opened. "I have to go for now, but I'll be back tomorrow."

Kat walked down the street to her car, head down, still angry at the world. Well, mostly just angry at God. Though she knew that anger was only the second step in the five stages of grief, she couldn't seem to move past it. Besides, bargaining was the next stage and what did she have to bargain with? It's not like God was going to bring Stella back to life. The time of those types of miracles had passed centuries ago. So, she stayed angry, but the rage was eating her inside. She'd lost five pounds from lack of eating and an intense desire to hit things flared up constantly. That's why she was heading to the gym currently.

Kat hoped the gym would have a class scheduled so someone would push her, but she would settle for the gym being open and allowing her to hit the bag. She didn't know their schedule well enough to know if they were even open, but as they weren't far, she decided the short drive would be worth it. She had picked up some cheap punching gloves at a Big 5 after the first workout and kept them in her car along with a top, leggings, and sports bra for whenever the urge might hit her. If she continued kickboxing, she knew she would eventually need other equipment, but she would attack that road when it appeared.

Glancing up to see how much further the car was—she thought she had parked closer—Kat stopped in her tracks. Though the neighborhood was not as bustling as some of the nearby up-and-coming neighborhoods, there were still quite a few people out walking the sidewalks, either pushing strollers or holding dog leashes. Two women, probably in their forties, who obviously exercised this way often by the rhythmic pumping of their arms, speed walked past Kat as she stood rooted to the spot. One appeared entirely normal, but the other was surrounded by a golden glow. The same glow she had seen around Stephanie earlier.

Kat blinked her eyes as they passed wondering if she

had imagined the light; she hadn't been sleeping well after all, but as she turned for a second glance, the light remained. Worse yet, a woman pushing a stroller was also surrounded by the light and a man jogging by with his Labrador exuded the same shine.

Kat rubbed her eyes. Am I going crazy? First the light around Stephanie and now light around total strangers. She continued the final few feet to her blue mini cooper. As she shut the door, she looked up again. No light surrounded any of the people in front of her now. She must have been dreaming. Starting the car, she continued to the gym, though her intense desire to hit something had been replaced with questions and confusion.

"Hey, glad to see you make it back in," Jason said as Kat walked past the desk.

"Yeah, it's been a rough week. I felt the need to hit something tonight. I'm really sorry about the other night." Though Kat was answering Jason, her eyes were scanning the gym, hoping no one else would be sporting the golden glow.

"Yeah, I hear that," he said, but Kat knew they were empty words. There was little chance his week had been as bad as hers. She nodded, so he wouldn't think she was ignoring him, before continuing to the locker room.

She changed into her workout clothes and pulled out the stiff, new gloves from her bag. With still ten minutes until class started, Kat sat down on one of the chairs off to the side to wait. A young girl with her blond hair pulled up in a ponytail sat down beside her and began to wrap her wrists in a long slightly stretchy fabric.

"Hi, I'm Lilly. You're new, right?"

Kat nodded, but her focus was on a boxer across the room. He had on a pair of headphones and a Batman shirt over black leggings. He looked unremarkable, except for the pale light surrounding him. "Do you see it?" she asked the girl next to her.

"See what?" The girl looked up and followed Kat's gaze.

"The glow." Her voice was barely a whisper as Kat pointed at the dark-skinned boxer who was bobbing and weaving across the room.

"Who Jon? Yeah, he's pretty amazing. I haven't been here long, but they say he's always had the gift."

But that hadn't been what Kat had meant, and she could tell from the girl's answer that she could not see the same shining light that Kat could. Jason called the class to order then, and Kat filed into line. But her eyes remained on the boxer. What made him different? Why did he have the light, but no one else did?

"See something you like?"

"What?" Lilly was staring at her, a smile tugging on the corners of her mouth.

"Jon, you've been staring at him for five minutes. I

know he's fun to watch, but he's going to think you have the hots for him." Her blond hair swung back and forth as she jogged in place next to Kat.

A blush colored Kat's cheek, and she forced her eyes from the glow. "No, it's not like that. It's—" she stopped. Had she been about to tell a total stranger about the lights? "He's just so good."

Kat made sure to keep her eyes from Jon the rest of the workout. It wasn't hard as he was working pads with the more advanced people and she was busy trying to remember her punches on the bag.

As soon as the workout was over, Kat grabbed her bag and rushed out of the gym. She was afraid to be caught staring at Jon again, and she didn't feel like answering any more questions. She wanted to find out what the light was. Between the light and the recent dreams, she felt like she was losing her mind.

Kat worked through options as she drove home. She could no longer ignore that something was happening to her, and she needed to tell someone. Her immediate thought was Patrick. Even though they hadn't been close before, Stella's death had thrown them together and created a bond of friendship, but he was dealing with his own problems with Maddie's latest breakdown.

There was Dr. Gibson, but she'd like to keep her craziness out of work. The last thing she needed was the wrong person finding out and her getting fired. And she didn't know him well. Maybe she should consider outside help. A psychiatrist she didn't know who would never see her again might be a good choice. At least that way she could pour out her feelings and maybe he or she would have some suggestions. That idea brought a semblance of peace to her jumbled thoughts, and as soon as she reached her apartment, she hurried in to use her laptop.

Opening the silver cover, she logged on and tapped her pink fingernail on the keys while it loaded. When the search bar appeared, she paused. Was this really the best option? Her fingers hovered over the keys just a moment longer before typing out the words Psychiatrist Olympia Washington.

A dozen sites popped up, all within fifteen miles. Not wanting something too close to home, Kat widened her search to thirty miles. A Christian site caught her eye and she clicked on it. Dr. Angela Gilead had been practicing for ten years. With light blond hair and blue eyes, her face seemed almost angelic and immediately called to Kat. After jotting down the address, Kat dialed the number on the website hoping they would have a slot available soon.

"Hello, Dr. Gilead's office, how may I help you?"

Kat swallowed. "Yes, hi. My name is Kat Jameson, and I was wondering if Dr. Gilead had any availability in the next few days?"

"Are you a current patient?" the woman on the other end asked.

"No, I just found her online." Kat bit her lip wondering if this was really the best decision.

"Very well. Please hold and I'll check for you."

Before Kat could respond, the phone clicked and hold music played in her ear. Maybe this hadn't been such a good idea. She was just about to hang up the phone when another voice came on.

"This is Dr. Gilead. Is this Kat?"

Kat blinked, surprised the doctor would get on the phone herself. "Yes, this is Kat."

"Well Kat, I had a cancellation for tomorrow afternoon. Would you be able to come at five?"

"Could you make it five thirty? I generally finish work around five, and I've taken a lot of time off recently."

"Absolutely, I can make that work; I will see you then."

Kat thanked the woman and hung up the phone. No turning back now.

"*Kat, I need you to listen.*"

"*Sure, Stella, what's up?*" *Kat looked up from the medical book she was reading to where Stella was folding laundry.*

"*The lights are important and you need to listen.*"

"*Lights?*" *Kat looked around, but the only lights on were the ones in the kitchen.* "*What lights, Stella?*"

"*The ones around the people. They are important. He needs you, Kat.*"

Kat's eyes popped open. This was the second night she had dreamed of Stella. While it was nice to see her friend again, the dreams held a certain intensity to them that set Kat's nerves on edge. Why were the lights so important and what was she supposed to be listening for? As she got out of bed, Kat hoped the psychiatrist would have answers this afternoon.

~

*D*r. Gilead's office was a small brick building at the edge of a strip mall. A simple white stencil of her name was the advertisement on the building. The inside was just as minimalist as the outside. A single brown desk, manned by a mousy brunette was the only furniture in the tan and beige room. Kat checked in with the woman, who immediately sent her back to the only other door, Dr. Gilead's office.

"Welcome Kat. Why don't you have a seat?" Dr. Gilead's voice flowed like silk over Kat's nerves and though she didn't know this woman, she felt at ease with her.

Nodding, she sat down on the tan settee and ran her hands down her linen clad thighs. The settee had a raised end, and Kat wondered if she was supposed to lie back or keep sitting. She glanced over at Dr. Gilead for a clue, but the woman was looking over some papers on a clipboard. Deciding to wait for a hint from the woman, she let her eyes wander around the cream-colored office.

The walls and carpet were nearly the same color of cream, the carpet just a shade darker. A few picture frames with licenses and awards hung about the office as well as a cross right behind the dark brown desk. Kat looked away from the symbol, still angry at God, though it struck her as odd that she had chosen a Christian psychiatrist.

Even more interesting was the fact there were no pictures in the office. None on the walls and none on the desk that Kat could see. Though she found that strange as Dr. Gilead appeared to be in her forties, she dismissed it as a woman married to her work. Kat knew that feeling well. Her last serious relationship was a year ago, and she kept no pictures in her office at work.

A small two-shelf bookshelf by the desk finished off the furniture in the room, other than the chair Dr. Gilead was sitting in and the settee that Kat occupied. It was a sparse office, but the outer office was the same. Must be a minimalist.

"If you're ready, why don't you lean back and tell me your problems," Dr. Gilead's voice broke into Kat's analysis of her.

"Okay." Kat reposed, trying to decide where to start. "Well, my best friend died last week from a burst aneurysm, and I guess I'm having trouble accepting it. I'm angry." The words flowed out of her mouth as she told the doctor about her past few weeks, her trouble sleeping and eating, and finally the odd light she was seeing.

"Interesting, so the light isn't around everyone?"

The pen scratching across the paper sent chills down

Kat's spine. For some reason, it felt out of place in the serene environment.

"No, it was only around some of the people I saw, but I have no idea why. There didn't seem to be any pattern. They weren't all men or all women; they weren't all young or all old. It seemed random." Though she tried to forget the images, they replayed in her head the rest of the night and like a puzzle, Kat tried to find some common denominator but always came up empty handed. There appeared to be no rhyme or reason for why some people emitted a shine and others didn't.

"Have you prayed about it?"

Startled, Kat's head snapped in Dr. Gilead's direction. "No, God and I aren't really on speaking terms right now. He took away my friend and left her daughter without a mother. He could have stopped it."

Dr. Gilead stared at her a moment. "It's interesting you chose a Christian counselor, then isn't it?"

Kat had no response. She wondered the same thing herself.

Dr. Gilead didn't wait for an answer before continuing. "God didn't cause her death; sin entering the world caused all the pain and hurt that God never intended for us."

"But He could stop it," Kat repeated. She needed it to be true.

"He can't take away our free will, but He speaks to us, hoping we will listen and follow His will."

"Are you saying she died because she didn't listen to God?" The anger surging through Kat's body colored her face and sent her pulse through the roof. She sat up, glaring at the doctor. Surely, she had misunderstood. No one believed God punished that way, did they?

Dr. Gilead's eyebrow rose, but the rest of her face remained stoic. "That is not what I am suggesting at all, but your reaction is intriguing. Do you remember the story of Jonah?"

Conflicting emotions battled within Kat. Rage, disbelief, confusion. Her hands clenched, her knuckles turning white as she gripped the settee. She wanted to flee, to throw something, to slap some emotion onto Dr. Gilead's face, but some force kept her sitting. "Of course, I remember Jonah. A giant fish swallowed him. What does that have to do with -"

"What do you think would have happened to the people of Nineveh if Jonah had continued to ignore God's word?"

Kat shook her head, bewildered. She didn't remember the rest of the story, just the part about the giant fish. How had they gotten onto Jonah anyway? "I don't know."

"God spared them only because Jonah finally told them of their rebellious ways and they repented. If Jonah had ignored God's voice, all of those in Nineveh would have perished."

A piece clicked into place, and a light went off in Kat's

head. "Are you saying that Stella might have been saved if someone else had been listening to God?" The words tumbled out slowly. They still made little sense to her. Wasn't that still like punishing people? Then a staggering memory flared in her mind. The church service where she had felt she needed to pray with Stella, but she hadn't. "Oh, my gosh, did I keep her from being saved?"

"What do you mean?"

"I," Kat struggled with the words, "I felt that I should pray with her the Sunday before she died, but I was too worried about what people would think, and I ignored it. Would God have healed Stella if I prayed with her?" A wave of guilt like she'd never felt before crashed over her.

"God didn't need you to pray to heal Stella, but it sounds like He wanted you to listen. Perhaps these lights are another way God is trying to speak to you. You might want to listen this time." Though spoken in the same monotonous voice the doctor had been using since Kat entered the room, these words held a hint of foreboding, and an involuntary shudder raced through Kat's body.

Suddenly the weight lifted from Kat's body, and she shot up off the settee. "You have no idea what you're talking about. I don't even know why I came here." Her body shook with the rage roiling through it.

Still no change of expression came across the doctor's face. "Perhaps one day you will."

"Ugh," Kat clenched her teeth, tamping down the

urge to grab the woman by the hair and shake her head back and forth until some emotion lit her deadpan expression. "You're crazy," she spat instead and yanked the door open, stomping out of the office and past the receptionist, who didn't appear disturbed in the least by this display. Was everyone a bunch of robots here?

The cool air outside slapped Kat as she opened the door. Though summer, a cold spell had settled on the interior in the last week and dropped the temperatures. Kat shivered as she rummaged in her purse for her keys. "Stupid, crazy woman," she muttered under her breath as her fingers finally touched the cold metal.

"Are you all right?"

Kat looked up to see a woman on the nearby sidewalk staring at her. *I must look insane.* "I'm fine. Just looking for my keys." She held them up in triumph and smiled at the woman, who nodded, but didn't look convinced.

After unlocking the car, Kat opened the door and sat in the driver's seat for a moment collecting her thoughts. Though still angry, she wondered if maybe Dr. Gilead had a point. There were other men and women in the Bible who delivered God's messages and saved people like Paul and the other apostles, but that was then. God didn't work that way now, did he? After all, He didn't speak to people through burning bushes or even audibly for all Kat knew; it was all just about relying on a feeling, wasn't it?

For as long as she'd been a Christian, she had never

heard God speak aloud to her, but then she had never been a devoted Christian if she thought about it. Sure, she went to church on Sundays, but she lived her own life during the week, giving little thought to God Monday through Saturday. Had she been missing something?

～

Tuesday, Texas

*J*ordan picked up the last box and took one final look around her apartment. She had packed up her valuable items and was taking them to her mother's house for the summer. A friend would be subletting the apartment for the rest of the summer. With a final deep breath—she was really trusting God on this one—she shut off the light with her elbow and pulled the door shut behind her.

With careful steps, she made her way down the stairs to the parking lot where Jess leaned against Jordan's car, hands under her large, pregnant belly. She looked as if her baby would be born any day. "Are you sure about this?"

After a little shuffling of the boxes, Jordan made room for the final box in the trunk and shut the lid. "I'm not sure about anything lately, but I told God I would follow His will, so I'm going to do my best." She and Jess had become friends through church. Though Amanda had been her initial contact, Jordan found she had more in common with Jess who hadn't grown up Christian either.

"But Washington state? Why would He possibly send you so far away?"

Jordan shrugged. "There's a woman there I need to help. I don't know much about her, but I'm sure God will tell me more along the way."

"You're braver than I think I could be," Jess said, "but I wish you didn't have to go alone. If this baby weren't due any day, I'd go with you."

Jordan smiled at her friend's good nature. "I know, and I appreciate it, but I'll be fine. God has a plan for this. Besides, I doubt Chad would let you get very far right now."

Jess blushed and rubbed her belly again. "He has become pretty protective of both of us. Please keep in touch though."

"I will, and you better tell me when you have that baby." Jordan hugged Jess, fighting the urge to unpack everything in her trunk and just stay. This was so out of her comfort zone. With a final glance at Jess, Jordan climbed in the driver seat and started the car. Her mother lived a few hours away, so she was spending the night with her and heading to the airport in the morning. Jordan waved to Jess and pulled out onto the street. No turning back now.

WEDNESDAY, TEXAS

*J*ordan stood just inside the airport and took a deep breath. Her mother had wanted to stay with her, but the airport wasn't that big, the line wouldn't be long, and it wasn't like Jordan was going to get lost, so she had told her mother just to drop her off curbside. However, now that she was here facing this journey alone, the nerves were surfacing again.

Closing her eyes, she took another calming breath and sent up her familiar prayer. "Lord, I don't know how I can be of use to you today, but please use me to do your will." Though barely audible, the words had an immediate calming effect on the tangled bundle in her stomach. She hoisted her bag further up her shoulder and headed toward the check-in counter.

Though small and certainly not busy, the chatter in

the airport was a constant hum as Jordan joined the short line to check her luggage. A couple was in front of her and Jordan smiled at their young child who kept peeking at her around her mother's leg. She lifted her hand in a wave, and the girl buried her blond curls in her mother's leg.

"Let's go, Sarah." Her mother gently pushed the little girl's back to turn her to the left. Jordan waved one last time before stepping up to the counter.

"Where are you headed?" The voice of the brunette was perky, but Jordan could see the beginning of dark circles under her eyes. She must not be sleeping well.

"Seattle." Jordan hoped some words of assurance for the woman would flood her mind, but none came. The woman tapped a few keys on the computer and printed off the label.

"Here you go, all set. Just take your luggage over there for scanning."

"Thank you." Jordan flashed a sincere smile hoping it might at least comfort the woman through the rest of the day.

After dropping her suitcase off and waiting through the security check line, Jordan headed to gate three. Abilene's airport was so small that there were only three gates, and only two operated on most days. The posting at the gate showed the plane on time. Jordan glanced at her watch, forty minutes to wait. Time enough to spend some time in the word and hope for some clarification of who she was looking for.

Jordan dropped her bag on the floor and sat in the black vinyl chair. She unzipped the back portion and felt around for her Bible. Her fingers touched the pebbled pattern and she pulled the book out. The pages flipped and she found herself in Jonah. As her eyes traveled across the lines, the words ignited a feeling in her chest that her mission was similar to Jonah's. Not that she was going to save an entire city of people from destruction, but that God was using her to fulfill some higher plan.

The boarding announcement for her plane interrupted her reading. Jordan sighed and shut the Bible. Surely clarity would come on the plane; she didn't want to think about what she was going to do if she landed in Seattle and still had no idea of what to do next. She zipped the bag back up and shuffled onto the plane with the rest of the passengers.

The flight out of Abilene was a small prop plane with one seat on one side of the aisle and two on the other. Jordan's seat was 13C, a little over halfway down and by the window. She slid the bag under the seat in front of her and settled into the small blue seat, fastening her seatbelt and turning off her phone. An older woman in a black pantsuit sat down in the seat next to her.

Jordan opened her mouth to greet her seatmate, but the scowl on the woman's face stopped her. The woman's eyes glanced her direction before returning to her phone where she furiously tapped her screen as the creases in her forehead deepened.

"You'll need to turn that off in ten minutes for lift off," the stewardess said as she passed Jordan's row.

"Yes, I just need to take care of this first." The woman answered but never lifted her eyes.

Though not uncommon these days, Jordan wondered how people could be so obsessed with their electronics. No wonder people couldn't hear God speaking to them any longer; they had replaced Him with an idol whether or not they realized it.

"Must be important," Jordan said softly.

"Excuse me?" The woman's voice cut like a sliver of glass, but Jordan didn't let that phase her.

"Whatever is on your phone. You haven't looked up from it since you sat down."

"I don't see what business that is of yours." The glare from the steely blue eyes was just as cutting as the voice had been.

Jordan shrugged. "It probably isn't, but I think there are more important things in the world than whatever problem you are dealing with on your phone."

"When you are a CEO and dealing with daily incompetency, then you can talk, but until then perhaps you should keep your opinion to yourself."

Jordan clenched her jaw to keep the spiteful words she

wanted to say from spewing forth. This woman didn't know what she had been through. To her, Jordan probably looked like the average carefree twenty-something that still lived at home and milked mommy and daddy for money. She would have no way of knowing of the encounter Jordan had survived last year or the years she had grown carrying a pregnancy to term and then giving the baby away. The ire that had been speeding her pulse dimmed as Jordan thought about this. Then she realized she had no way of knowing the woman's situation either. Perhaps whatever was on her phone was important. She closed her eyes, asking forgiveness for her assumptions and prayers for the woman next to her.

The pre-recorded take off speech came on over the loudspeaker, and the woman cursed under her breath as she rapidly tapped a few more buttons. The stewardess shot a warning look at the lady as she demonstrated how to fasten and unfasten the seat belts.

Jordan leaned over and whispered to the woman. "I think she wants you to put the phone away." She didn't want to enrage her seatmate any more, but she didn't want the stewardess singling them out with her anger either.

"Just another minute," the woman seethed, her fingers still flying across the face of the phone.

Jordan placed a hand on the woman's arm and suddenly she was transported back almost a year ago to the similar experience she had with Amanda. The surrounding noise stopped; even the woman's fingers paused on the phone. She looked up, locking eyes for the first time with Jordan. "It can wait." Though the words came out of Jordan's mouth, she didn't feel as if they were her own. The woman's eyes widened and just like before, Jordan felt a jolt of electricity. *It's weird being on the other side this time.*

As quickly as it came, the moment disappeared and the stewardess's speech once again reached Jordan's ears. The woman's eyes held Jordan's just a moment longer before returning to her phone. Her finger hovered over the screen, but then moved to the top and powered the phone down.

"What was that?" Questions hovered in her eyes.

Jordan opened her mouth to answer, but before she could utter a word, a bright light flooded her vision and then an image filled her mind. A raven-haired teenage girl lay on a pink bedspread. Her skin was ashen, but bright pools of red spread out from her wrists. A straight-edged razor lay near her right hand and a white paper resided near her left. An involuntary shudder coursed through Jordan as the picture in her mind zoomed in on the note. 'Because no one was ever there for me' was scrawled in a shaky cursive across it. Darker spots dotted the paper. Tears? Then it was gone, and the seatmate came back into view.

For the first time, Jordan really looked at the woman. Creases ran across her forehead and out the sides of her eyes. Gray hairs were sprinkled among her dark hair along her temple. The blue eyes that stared at Jordan were exact copies of the hollow eyes Jordan had just seen in her mind. "Do you have a daughter?" Jordan had to push the words out over the large lump in her throat.

The woman narrowed her eyes, probably debating how much to tell a total stranger. Jordan was sure she would have denied it if it hadn't been for the shared moment. "I do," the woman said finally. "Why do you ask?"

Jordan took a deep breath, wondering what would be the best way to share her vision. *Lord please give me the right words.* "I don't know where you're going, but you need to see your daughter as soon as possible and tell her that you care and that you are there for her."

A hardness descended on the woman and she stiffened visibly. "What do you mean? I'm always there for my daughter."

"You don't know me and you have no reason to believe me, but I sometimes get visions about people. I just saw your daughter with a suicide note. I'm not saying you aren't there for her, but she feels like no one is."

The woman shook her head. "You're lying. I don't know why you'd want to make up a story like that, but you're sick." She turned away from Jordan, crossing her arms and craning her neck to scan the plane, probably looking for the stewardess to ask if she could change seats.

"Your daughter has dark hair like you and the same blue eyes, and the bedspread in her room is pink." The words were little more than a whisper, but the woman froze. Her head swiveled slowly back to Jordan.

"Lucky guess," the woman said, but her words were not as forceful as before. A note of fear came through.

"She has a purple butterfly tattoo on her left wrist."

That was enough to convince the woman. Her eyes darted back and forth as she took in every inch of Jordan's face. "Who are you? What do you want?"

Jordan shook her head, her blond hair fanning out around her face. "I'm nobody, and I want nothing. I don't even know why God picked me for this gift. I didn't even believe in Him until a few months ago. Honestly, I'm just trying to do what I feel He's telling me, and the vision he showed me is that your daughter is in trouble."

"Is it too late? Will I make it home in time to stop her?" The fear coating the woman's voice now was so different from her haughty attitude when she boarded. Jordan's heart went out to her, and she wished she could soothe her fears, but she wasn't getting anything else.

"I don't know," Jordan said honestly, "but I can't imagine God would show me this if it were too late to do anything about it."

Though the woman nodded, she did not appear

convinced. Her right thumb and index finger twisted the sparkly diamond ring on her left hand around and around. The woman's lips pursed, and Jordan waited for the question she knew was coming.

"Why me?" the woman whispered. "I don't even go to church. I'm always too busy."

Jordan smiled. "He knows you, even if you don't know Him yet. He's been knocking at your door wanting you to open it and let him inside. He wants to offer you peace."

The woman's eyes dropped to her lap. "I don't know if I can change. It's all I've ever known."

Jordan touched the woman's arm to get her to raise her eyes. "Not by yourself you can't, but with God's help, you can do anything."

When the woman placed her hand on top of Jordan's and asked to hear more about God, a feeling of peace radiated through Jordan. She had never led someone to Christ, but the words flowed like a river out of her mouth.

The plane landed, and the women hugged goodbye. As Jordan was exiting the plane, the stewardess reached out and touched her arm. "I've never seen such a transformation in a person in such a short time. What did you do?"

"Oh, it wasn't me." Jordan shook her head at the woman. "It was God."

The stewardess nodded, a small knowing smile tugging

at her own lips. "Have a safe stay," she said as Jordan waved and headed up the ramp.

As the terminal opened into the busy airport, Jordan shrank back. The Dallas airport was a sea of people, the current flowing rapidly both directions. This was not her first flight, but it was the first time she had flown alone into such a major hub. She gripped her bag tightly as she craned her neck, trying to find the large display boards that would tell her which gate to go to next.

When she finally saw the large black screens, Jordan stepped into the current and was jostled down the hallway. The gathering of people at the screen created a tide pool effect and Jordan stepped out of the current to keep herself from being pushed past her destination. She scanned the alphabetical destination cities until she found Seattle. C7; she would need to take the shuttle to a different terminal. Sighing, she stepped back into the stream of people and continued down, her eyes scanning the signs for the shuttle.

The hallway leading to the shuttle stop was less busy and Jordan breathed a sigh of relief. The cacophony of so many conversations all around her began to create a pounding in her head. Following the signs, she headed up the stairs and waited for the announcement that the train was approaching.

The doors hissed open and Jordan secured a seat, relaxing for a moment. Though the car was mostly full,

the ride was quiet, and Jordan watched the airport scenery
fly by. Too soon the train stopped and Jordan stepped out,
dreading the bustle that was sure to be in terminal C.
Again, the signs were her guide as she made her way down
the hallway. Thankfully, the hallways opened on gate C10
and Jordan only had to ride the current a few feet to
reach C7.

Though she was early, the chairs in the waiting area
were already filled with other people. Jordan spotted two
empty by the window and carefully made her way to
them. Just as she reached the black vinyl chairs, a man sat
in the chair next to her. She looked up into mesmerizing
green eyes.

"Oh, sorry, were you saving it?"

Jordan's breath caught in her throat. She hadn't
been interested in any man since the run in with
Trevor over a year ago, in fact she had avoided most
men, but this man was possibly the most handsome
man she had ever seen, and her normal reclusive
reaction didn't flare. His dark hair held a bit of wave
and his lips were the perfect shade of pink surrounded
by dark stubble. A clear cleft in his chin accented
chiseled cheekbones. He stared at her, waiting for an
answer. "No, it's fine," Jordan managed to say. "I'm not
saving it; I was just trying to get away from the
crowds."

His lips pulled back in a smile, revealing perfectly

white teeth. "I hear you. I'm from a small town myself, and I hate big crowds."

Jordan nodded, not wanting to tempt the tremor surging inside her appearing in her voice.

"Where are you headed?" the man continued, seeming oblivious to the effect he was having on Jordan.

"Seattle," she said softly, hoping her voice wouldn't give away the pounding in her chest. Why did she feel so comfortable talking to this total stranger?

His smile grew a little more. "Me too. I just graduated from Baylor, and I'm flying out to visit a friend of my dad to see if management is a good fit for me."

"I finished my sophomore year at Texas Tech," Jordan replied. Her heart was resuming its normal pace in her chest and her confidence was returning. "I'm studying to be a social worker."

"Wow, that's noble." The way his green eyes widened and stared even closer at her sent her heart thudding once again. "I'm Jeremy." He held out his hand to shake hers.

Jordan wanted to touch it, an odd feeling as she normally avoided contact with men, but she wanted to see if the electricity she felt in the air would travel down her arm causing the hair on her arms to stand up. What if her hand shook though? What if what she thought was a mutual interest was just friendly banter to pass the time? Mustering her courage, she clasped his hand with her own, enjoying the strong masculinity that radiated from the pressure he asserted on her hand and the brief spark of electric current that ran up her arm. "I'm Jordan." A slight widening of his eyes before he dropped his gaze to their hands told her that he had felt a similar jolt.

He cleared his throat as he released her hand. "So, what are you doing in Seattle?"

Jordan furrowed her brow. She didn't want to tell him the whole reason, at least not yet; it was too complicated to explain, so she settled for a half truth. "I'm visiting a friend." In his eyes, she could tell he wanted to ask her more about that, but after a moment he changed the topic and asked her about school instead.

She answered the questions, bartering with a few of her own, and by the time the announcement came over the loudspeaker for their plane, she felt as if she had known him for days instead of a few hours. They stood and shuffled into the group of people herding into a single line. As Jeremy pulled his ticket out, Jordan glanced down at the information and was disappointed to see that their seats weren't close together.

"I guess this will be goodbye," she said pointing down at Jeremy's ticket, "I'm about seven rows behind you."

His shoulders sank slightly as a flash of disappointment crossed his features. "Maybe we can trade seats with someone, but if not, can we meet after? I know it might sound strange, but I'd like to stay in touch. Maybe trade emails?" His eyes pleaded silently with her.

Jordan smiled at him, surprised at the words that tumbled out of her mouth. "I'd like that."

The line surged forward and they handed their tickets to the gate agent before continuing up the ramp. Inside, the plane was already half full. A couple was sharing the row with Jeremy, so Jordan continued to her own seat, a little disappointed that they wouldn't be able to continue their conversation.

As she buckled her seatbelt though, the reason for her journey flashed before her eyes and Jordan's mood shifted. She was about to land in an unknown city with no direction; she needed to spend this flight in prayer and hope that God revealed the next step to her. Though she had enjoyed getting to help the woman on the earlier flight, she was relieved that her seatmates, a pair of blond girls, were too engrossed in their own conversation to pay her much attention.

Jordan grabbed the Bible from her bag, relishing the feel of security that flooded her at the touch and closed her eyes. *Lord, I need to know what to do next. Please show me your will.*

~

*A*s Jordan stepped off the plane and into the Seattle airport, Jeremy waved at her. A flicker of warmth stirred in her heart, and Jordan couldn't help the smile that plastered itself across her face or the soft blush that followed it.

"How was the flight for you?" Jeremy asked when she reached his side. Together they walked down the terminal, dodging the onslaught of people scurrying in the other direction.

"It was good. My seatmates were friends, so it was quiet for me. How about for you?"

Jeremy smiled, but rolled his eyes. "I wasn't as lucky as you. The man next to me was a dipper and kept spitting in a cup. The smell was bad, but the sound was worse. Just a constant drip like a leaky faucet."

Jordan wrinkled her nose and shivered at the image. She had briefly dated a boy in high school who dipped, but the first time he had tried to kiss her, she nearly heaved up her lunch at the smell. The relationship ended after that. "I'm sorry, that sounds awful.

His shoulders rose in a shrug. "It wasn't my best flight, but it wasn't my worse either. At least he didn't talk my ear off." He grabbed her hand and pulled her left down a hall, following the signs for the baggage claim.

Jordan couldn't tear her eyes from their clasped hands as she followed him down the hall. She hadn't let a man even touch her since Trevor and she barely knew Jeremy, but it didn't feel wrong.

The baggage claim area was no less busy than the terminal had been, but it was a lot bigger than the one in

Abilene. Jordan's eyes widened as the room seemed to stretch forever. Large screens like the ones to announce arrivals and departures dotted the ends of the room. Jordan counted at least ten baggage carousels, but was sure there were more. Jeremy stopped in front of one of the screens and scanned the listings. He seemed to know his way around the airport.

"We're at carousel twelve." He tugged on Jordan's hand.

Jordan followed, but the crowd was getting to her. She wasn't normally claustrophobic, but there were so many people here; she felt like an ant in a sea of giants, and the hum of competing conversations created a buzzing in her bones.

As Jeremy stopped in front of one of the carousels, a red light flashed and a buzzer sounded. The conveyor belt coughed to life, and the crowd of people pushed against them, clamoring to find a spot around the circular conveyor. Colorful bags began their slow descent down the raised ramp, thudding at the bottom.

"What color is your bag?" Jeremy dropped her hand and shouldered forward a little into the crowd.

"Purple." Jordan raised her voice to be heard over the rival noise. She moved closer to Jeremy, missing the warmth from his hand. Her eyes scanned the luggage circling lazily in front of them, and she tugged his sleeve when her suitcase made its appearance.

He hoisted the dark purple suitcase off, handing it back to her before turning back to the belt in search of his own.

Jordan stood, unsure if she should stay or go. She wanted to speak a little longer with him, but felt self-conscious waiting on a man she barely knew, even if he was an oddly calming influence in the crowd of unknown.

Jeremy reached forward, grabbing a midnight blue suitcase. He turned and smiled at Jordan. "Oh good, you waited. I was hoping,"–he bit his perfect lip and looked down at the floor before bringing his green eyes up to meet Jordan's again– "that we might exchange numbers?"

The surrounding commotion seemed to fade as Jordan focused on his hopeful eyes. "I'd like that."

Jeremy's breath rushed out of his mouth and a smile stretched across his face. Taking her hand again, he led the way to a small concave, out of the rush of traffic. The noise was dimmer, and Jordan's tense muscles relaxed minutely. He pulled out his phone and handed it to her. Jordan reciprocated, digging her own phone out of her jean pocket.

"So where does your friend live?" Jeremy asked, as they switched phones back.

"Olympia," Jordan offered, remembering the vision of the capitol building. She had received no new visions on the plane, so she trusted she hadn't been wrong about that.

His shoulders sagged slightly. "Oh, well, I guess this is goodbye for now then. I'm staying at a local hotel tonight and meeting my dad's friend downtown tomorrow."

Jordan's spirit sank as well. The disappointment at leaving Jeremy was part of it, but the reality of the lonely journey ahead of her was also weighing on her. She had enjoyed having someone to talk to. "At least we can stay in touch now, though."

"That's true," he said, brightening. "Now I assume you need a ride?" He paused allowing Jordan time to nod. "Great, let's go find out when the shuttle leaves. I'll stay with you until then."

After securing her a seat on the next van, Jeremy led her to a bench. They sat and shared stories of their families. Jeremy spoke so vividly of his parents and brother and sister that Jordan felt she would recognize them on sight.

"What about your family?" he asked.

Jordan paused, thinking back to her mother's pushing her to terminate her pregnancy, but she kept that information to herself for now. "Well, my mother and I don't always see eye to eye, but they're good people. I have a younger sister who still lives at home with my parents."

"Van's here," the attendant called from the counter.

Jeremy's mouth pulled into a tight line, mimicking the regret Jordan felt inside as she wished they had more time. They stared at each other, awkwardness and electricity colliding in the space between them. It was too soon to kiss though Jordan was sure he wanted to as much as she did or thought she did. Her emotions were a roller coaster inside her. She didn't want this to be like Trevor. A part of her wanted to grab his phone and destroy it so he wouldn't have a way to contact her, but the other part of her wanted to see him again. She didn't destroy his phone because he grabbed her hands and squeezed them tightly. Romeo and Juliet flashed into her mind, and Jordan had finally understood Juliet's silly line about two palms kissing.

"I'll text you soon," Jeremy said, dropping her hands.

Jordan nodded, a shy smile on her lips. Then she grabbed her bag and boarded the van. The window seat in the second row beckoned to her, and she slid in, shooting Jeremy another wave.

A body crammed against her, breaking the moment, and Jordan looked up to find a man with a large belly struggling to buckle the seatbelt next to her. She slid a little closer to the window to give him more room, and after a few jabs to her ribs with his meaty elbows, he finally succeeded. Even with his arms crossed on his chest, more of him touched Jordan than she would have liked.

A family with a small child, blissfully sleeping, crawled in behind them and the van door shut. Jordan wasn't even sure how long of a drive it was to Olympia, but she figured she better turn to God again for more direction.

Wandering the streets of an unknown city held no appeal. Closing her eyes, she cleared her mind and tried to focus on listening.

Though the van was packed, no one said a word on the ride, allowing Jordan to enjoy the silence. *Patrick O'Donnell.* The name blazed in her mind, a marquis in white light. She had been expecting the name of the dark-haired woman. Who was Patrick? Was he related to the woman? Would he know where to find her? Trusting that God wouldn't lead her astray, Jordan settled back and enjoyed the rest of the ride.

∼

*T*he shuttle dropped Jordan off at the downtown Best Western in Olympia. As it drove away, she realized she should have asked him to stay as she had no idea if the hotel would even have a room for the night. Sighing, she opened the front door and looked around. A man around her age sat behind the front desk; his eyes focused on the flat screen TV playing on the other side of the room.

"Hi," Jordan said, approaching the desk. "I wanted to know if you have a room for tonight."

The man dragged his eyes from the TV screen to glance over at her. "Let me look." He typed a few things into his computer and then turned his bored eyes back on her. "I have a single available. It will be $100 for the night."

Jordan tried not to blanch at the amount. This was going to be an expensive trip, but she figured God would take care of her finances. She pulled out her credit card, generally used only for emergencies, and slid it across the desk.

The man tapped a few more keys, swiped her card, and then handed her a printed sheet of paper to sign. "Check out is at noon," he said, his eyes returning to the TV screen.

"I'll probably be staying for a few days," Jordan said as she signed the sheet. "Will I have to let you know?"

He clicked the computer screen again. "No, it looks open for now. I'll mark your room as taken until you check out then."

"Thanks." Jordan grabbed the receipt and the key card. Room 103 was just down the hallway.

Jordan dropped her bag on the full-sized bed, sending a tremor through the flowers on the bedspread. The room wasn't much—a small nightstand, dresser, and a table and chair the only other furniture in the room. The black screen of the TV filled one wall and a few pictures of fields of flowers hung on the other walls. It wasn't home, but it would work for as long as she needed to stay here.

Sitting down next to her bag, she pulled out her phone and pulled up the internet search. She typed in the white page search and then tapped in Patrick O'Donnell's name. Thankfully it wasn't a popular name and only one pulled up, but it listed only a phone number under the name, no address. What was she going to do now? She couldn't just call the man and ask if he knew a sad, dark-haired woman. Even if he didn't think she was crazy, he wouldn't go offering his friend's information to a total stranger. Sighing, she closed her eyes and rubbed her hand across the bridge of her nose. Why was God being so cryptic with this one?

WEDNESDAY

Stella visited Kat's dreams once again Wednesday morning, and she saw at least three people with the light throughout the day. Even worse, the guilt of not praying for Stella was weighing on her. Kat kept a stoic face on when visiting her patients, but she broke down every time she returned to her office.

When she'd left Dr. Gilead's office yesterday, she had thought the woman was crazy, but now there was a need to go back, to have her explain her cryptic messages. She laid her head on her desk and wondered if she would ever be okay again.

"All right, let's go."

"Go where?" Kat looked up to Dr. Gibson's warm eyes oozing concern. He had given her a few days of space, but now it appeared he was back.

"Where ever you need to go. I don't know you well, but you are obviously struggling with something."

"How do you know?" Kat hoped he would just leave her to stew in her own head.

"Because I called your name three times before I walked in here. Look, you are dealing with Stella's death, but something else is going on, and it's affecting your work. If I'm noticing, then others are too."

"It's nothing," Kat said, shaking her head and trying to convince herself as much as him.

"Sorry, but I'm not taking no for an answer. There is something going on, and with everything you've been through recently, you could use a friend, so I'll ask you again, where are we going?"

Kat stared at him a moment longer, debating whether to keep pushing him away or just let him tag along. He didn't have to come in with her when they got there. "All right, we're going for a drive then, I guess."

He smiled as she grabbed her jacket and her keys.

"So, where is this drive taking us?" he asked as Kat pulled out of the parking lot.

"To see a shrink." Dr. Gibson's eyebrows knitted together, but Kat refused to reveal any more. Deciding not to press the issue, he pulled out his phone, presumably to check his emails, and they drove the rest of the way in silence.

Thirty minutes later, Kat pulled into the parking lot she had left less than forty-eight hours ago and stopped.

"It can't be," she said softly.

"What?" Dr. Gibson put his phone down and glanced around.

"It's gone," Kat stammered. Though the building she had been in was still there, no one had been in it for some time. The windows were boarded up and spray painted over. She blinked, not believing her eyes. "Yesterday, an office stood here. I went inside. I sat on a couch."

"It doesn't look like there's been an office here for some time," Dr. Gibson said slowly.

"Don't you think I can see that?" Kat snapped. Her heart thrummed loudly in her chest. "I'm telling you though that yesterday there was a business here."

"Kat, you've been under a lot of stress…"

"Don't patronize me," Kat yelled, cutting him off. "I am not crazy. I know what I saw." But suddenly she wasn't so sure. Had she imagined the meeting? Her hands shook against the steering wheel, and her vision blurred.

"Hey, it's okay." Dr. Gibson placed a hand on hers. "You lost your best friend."

"But… I…" Kat stammered, but no coherent thought came out of her mouth. Was she going crazy?

"Here, let's change places, and I'll drive back." He was being so kind that Kat didn't have the heart to argue. She placed the car in park and unstrapped her seatbelt. As she opened the door, she couldn't resist the urge to get a closer look at the building.

"I'll be right back," she said as he came around her blue mini cooper.

She took a step toward the building, then another. A slat in the boards allowed her a peek inside the building. Though dark, the shape looked the same, but there was no furniture and the wall paper was peeling. It didn't look like anyone had used this building in years.

"I know what I saw," Kat whispered to herself and crossed to the doorway. She had hoped to see an old name, but the boards completely covered the entrance. Sighing, she turned back to the car. Dr. Gibson stood at the driver's side door watching her.

Ignoring his questioning gaze, she opened the passenger door, sat down, and folded her hands in her lap. Kat had always felt in control in her life, but suddenly everything she had known was spiraling out of control.

Dr. Gibson, to his credit, said nothing; he simply started the car and turned it around.

Kat sat in silence for half the drive, but finally she could contain the question no longer. "Do you believe God talks to us?"

His eyes focused on her for just a second before turning back to the road. "Of course I do. Why do you think I started talking to you?"

"What?" Kat hadn't been expecting that response at

all. She'd been prepared for him to say yes. Or to tell her she was crazy. But she was not prepared for that response.

He chuckled. "Kat, I've been a believer a long time, but I didn't start listening until recently. Can I tell you my story?"

Kat nodded and he continued. "I've been at my gym for several years. I go to work out, but I've talked to people and they know I have faith. Last Christmas, a girl at our gym died in a car accident. She and her whole family, actually. The gym manager was close to her, and he pulled me aside one day to ask me why God would let bad things happen to good people."

Kat's mouth dropped open. How could his story be so like hers?

"I didn't have an answer for him that day. I don't even know if she was a believer, but I asked other Christians and researched on my own. As I did that, I grew closer to God, and I felt this urging to say things to people and do things for them. I realized then I was hearing that still, small voice they talk about. One that I had probably heard for a long time, but never really listened for. Do you know what I mean?"

Kat nodded, and the guilt pressed down even harder. "I think I felt that urging to pray with Stella, but I ignored it. Do you think Stella died because I ignored it?"

Dr. Gibson shook his head. "I don't know if it works like that, but I do think God can't use us if we aren't obedient, and I think maybe he was asking you to be obedient."

Kat curled up in her seat, but she let his words wash over her. Was God asking her to be obedient? And if He was, could she be?

~

*K*at stared at Patrick across the table, relieved that he had let her come over, but unsure where to begin.

"Kat, what is going on with you?" Patrick's stance was defensive, his arms crossed over his chest.

Her finger traced an imaginary pattern on the table top as she tried to think of the right words to tell him. "I think I might be going insane," she whispered, dragging her eyes up to meet his.

He rolled his eyes. "What are you talking about?"

"I'm angry all the time, and I can't seem to stop it. Then the other night I saw a light around people. I went to a psychiatrist who told me maybe it was God talking to me, which made me even angrier so I left." She knew she was rambling, but she couldn't stop the words from falling out of her mouth, nearly tripping over each other in their effort to get out.

"Then I went back with Dr. Gibson and it was gone. Well, not gone, but the building was boarded over and hadn't been used in a long time, but I was there on a couch. I wondered why her walls were so bare, but I thought she was a minimalist. I'm not even sure if the building ever was Dr. Gilead's place because I couldn't see a sign, but I was there. I didn't imagine it." She pursed her lips together, forcing her words to stop and waited for his reaction. Her green eyes pleaded with him to believe her, to understand.

His eyes narrowed as they searched her face. She had known Patrick for years and while they had never been close, he knew her well enough to know when she was lying. He ran a hand through his copper hair as his breath gushed out. "I'm not sure why you told me this or what you want me to do about it."

"I want you to tell me I'm not crazy," Kat cried, then remembering Maddie was still sleeping she lowered her voice. "I needed you to understand why I've been so angry."

"I don't think you're crazy," he said leaning forward, "I think you're just stressed, and we're all angry, but you need to find a healthier way to deal with it. I know you want to be around Maddie, but she's suffering too and she needs a strong role model, not an angry one."

Kat laid her head on the table. "I know. I don't want to be so angry, but I don't know how to make it go away. I even joined a boxing gym. It's helping a little, but not enough."

Patrick sighed. "Well, I don't think you'll want to hear this, but I think you need to give it to God. I was angry too. Now, I'm a single parent and I lost the love of my life, but I knew I needed to be strong for Maddie. It's an everyday thing, but I pray each morning for healing and hope, and it gets me through the day. God understands our anger, but maybe if you try talking with Him, He'll show you a way to heal."

Kat bit her lip. She wanted to believe Patrick; she was tired of being so angry all the time. "Do you believe me? About the psychiatrist, I mean?" She didn't know why, but she needed Patrick to believe her. She needed someone to believe she wasn't crazy because she was no longer so sure herself.

"I can't explain that, but I believe you believe what you saw. Could you have gotten the address wrong the second time?"

She lifted her head enough to shake it back and forth. Tears pricked her eyes. Even if God could soothe her anger, what was she going to do about this?

"Hey, it will be okay," Patrick's voice was softer as he reached out a hand to touch her arm. "I'm sure there is an explanation for it."

"Yeah, like I've lost my mind," Kat mumbled. Patrick cast empathetic eyes on her, but it was clear he didn't know what else to say. Though she wasn't quite ready to go home alone yet, Kat felt she was close to wearing out her welcome. So, after thanking Patrick for listening to her and making him promise to tell Maddie she would be back soon, Kat gathered her purse and keys, gave Patrick an awkward hug, and headed out to her car.

She buckled the seatbelt and then paused, mulling over Patrick's words and Dr. Gibson's from earlier. Would God really be open to her venting at him? Kat didn't see that she had much of a choice. Talking to the psychiatrist hadn't helped and she didn't want to try another. Placing her hands on the wheel, Kat took a deep breath and opened her mouth.

"God, if you're listening, I'm still angry with you. I think you could have saved Stella, and I can't understand why you didn't, but the anger is eating me up." She paused, deciding what to say next. She wasn't sure if you were supposed to bargain with God, but it was the first thing that came to mind. "Okay, God. I don't know why you want me, but you have my attention. Help me listen, and I'll do whatever you need."

Kat wasn't sure if she should say more and she felt silly speaking aloud in her car, so she left it at that and waited to see if God would answer her.

THURSDAY

The sunlight streaming in the windows woke Jordan. Blinking against the intruding light, she rubbed her eyes and stretched her arms. She hadn't thought she would sleep well in a bed not her own, but it had sucked her right in and she had fallen asleep before she had even finished praying.

Her phone chimed and she fished it off the nightstand. The bright glare of the screen hurt her still-adjusting eyes. She rubbed them again and the screen came into focus. A message from Jeremy filled the screen.

It was nice to meet you. I hope your first night was a good one—Jeremy.

Jordan bit her lip. It had been nice, but now she had the extra task of trying to find this Patrick O'Donnell. She typed back a quick reply, dressed, and headed down for breakfast.

There were only a few people in the breakfast area. A couple with two small children, munching on donuts, filled one table, and an older gentleman in a plaid shirt sat at another table reading a newspaper.

Jordan scooped some scrambled eggs from the silver container onto her plate, hoping they wouldn't taste as plastic as they looked. She added a few slices of crispy bacon that looked like someone had left them in the pan just a minute too long, and an orange. At least that would be edible.

She chose one of the smaller tables, setting her plate down before returning to the continental buffet to grab a cup of juice.

After praying, she scooped up a forkful of eggs. They were sandpaper in her mouth, and it took all of Jordan's willpower to finish chewing and not spit them out. The bacon wasn't much better, and Jordan knew she'd have to find real food. She finished her coffee and gathered her plates to throw away. A tiny twinge of guilt pricked her conscience as she tossed the leftover food away, but one could hardly call what tumbled into the trashcan food.

Jordan exited the hotel and glanced around. She had chosen a hotel downtown to be able to walk places, but downtown here differed greatly from back in Lubbock.

Though summer, it was cooler in Washington than Texas. A light layer of goosebumps broke out on her arms, and she wished she had brought a jacket. Guitar music reached her ears, and she turned to find the source. A man sitting in a nearby doorway had pulled out a guitar and was strumming. His ratty hair made Jordan wonder when his last bath had been. She stepped a little closer to the street as she continued down the sidewalk.

A small café with outdoor seating appeared on her left and Jordan coughed as she walked through an unfamiliar smelling cloud of smoke. *Is that pot?* She had heard they had legalized it here, but had never expected to see people smoking it out in public. *Was that even legal?* Her pace quickened as the feeling of being out of her element increased.

Two men, dressed all in black, coming her direction sent her heart racing. Instinctively, she pulled her purse just a little tighter to her side and wished she had someone familiar with her. Though she was healing, her faith in people, men especially, had been broken last year and fear of their motives often coursed through her mind.

Jordan continued down the sidewalk, shocked at the number of homeless people sleeping in doorways or on benches. Did they have no shelters here? "God, please help these people," she whispered, wishing she had the finances to help.

After about a block, Jordan found herself in a small

café. A few older people sat at the bar reading newspapers and drinking coffee, but the quaint tables covered in a red-checkered pattern were all empty. Jordan chose one near a window and waited for a menu.

As the waitress approached, another vision filled Jordan's head. She was the dark-haired woman, seeing the world through her eyes. As she walked, she saw a glow around people. Not everyone, but a few in every direction she turned. *What does it mean?*

"The lights are My angels protecting those who need to hear." Though not audible, Jordan felt the voice in her head. "She needs to see."

"Miss, are you okay?"

Jordan's body unfroze and she turned to look up at the waitress whose brown eyes were wide with concern. She appeared about forty with gray hairs creeping in around her otherwise dark temple. Her hair was pulled back in a messy bun that looked effortless and professional at the same time. Worry lines stood out on her face and forehead, and the pencil in her right hand hovered just over the white pad she held in her left.

"I'm fine." Jordan offered a smile to assure the woman. "I was just thinking about something. Sorry if I scared you."

The woman clearly did not believe that story as she set the menu on the table instead of handing it to Jordan, but she didn't press the issue. Jordan was sure she dealt with colorful characters on a regular basis.

"Okay, if you're sure." A note of apprehension still resided in her voice. "Can I get you something to drink?"

"Hot chocolate, please." Jordan broadened her smile which seemed to work as the woman, whose name tag read Paula, smiled back. Her shoulders released from their fight or flight tensing and dropped a few inches giving the woman a more relaxed stance before she turned to put the drink order in.

Jordan picked up the menu and perused the contents. She wanted something filling in case she didn't have time for lunch, so she decided on an omelet with a side of pancakes.

When Paula returned with the steaming hot cocoa, Jordan placed her breakfast order and then wrapped her hands around the powder blue mug. Though Jordan liked coffee, she was particular in how she would drink it. Growing up in Texas, she hadn't had it very much, though her father drank it every morning. He, however, drank it black.

One morning, when she had been particularly curious about the taste, he had offered her a sip of his, but she had spat it out before even swallowing it. It tasted like burnt water. Years later in high school, a friend introduced her to mochas and that was all Jordan could drink. As her friend,

Marie, always chided her, Jordan liked her coffee tan, not black.

Unfortunately, most restaurants couldn't get a mocha right. It always ended up tasting too much like coffee, so Jordan would order teas or hot chocolates and save her coffee cravings for shops that specialized in them.

As Jordan brought the lip of the cup to her lips to blow on it, she thought about the vision. If this woman was seeing this light that meant she had a gift like Jordan's. Did she know what to make of the light? Something told Jordan she didn't; she was probably just as lost as Jordan had been when her visions had started.

She took a sip, letting the liquid infuse her body with warmth as it traveled down her throat and into her stomach. The bell above the door jingled and Jordan glanced up to see a man with copper colored hair enter with a little blond girl.

"Hey, Patrick, Maddie. Grab a seat, and I'll be there shortly," Paula said to the pair before placing a plate in front of Jordan. Jordan thanked the woman, but her eyes were on the father-daughter duo. Could this be the Patrick she sought? It would be an extraordinary coincidence, but not out of God's power.

His eyes caught her for a second, and she knew he was indeed the man she was looking for. But how was she supposed to approach him? Jordan dropped her eyes to pray for both the food and wisdom. Then she ate her breakfast.

When the bill came, she wrote 'God Loves You' on the receipt, not really knowing why but feeling the need to, and gave Paula a few extra dollars. She wished she had more because she got the feeling that Paula could use it, if the stress lines on her face were any indication, but Jordan didn't know how long she might be called to stay here, and she wanted to make sure she would have enough to do God's will.

Now for the tough part. The man and girl, obviously his daughter, had just ordered their food, so Jordan felt this would be the best time to approach him. Still her stomach knotted at the prospect. What if he thought she was crazy and called the cops? She couldn't very well complete her task from jail, but if she left, she might not get another chance to talk to him. God had opened the door and since she was already walking on faith, she might as well trust Him here too.

"Excuse me, are you Patrick O'Donnell?"

His head cocked and his eyes narrowed. "Do I know you?"

Jordan opened her mouth, but words failed her. What could she possibly say?

"Daddy, I'm hungry. When is the food coming?" The little girl looked up from her coloring paper.

"In a minute, Maddie." His eyes never left Jordan's. "Tell me how you know my name."

Jordan bit her lip and clutched the strap of her purse tighter. "You wouldn't believe me."

"Try me."

His eyes never left hers, and after a deep breath, Jordan opened her mouth to continue. "Okay, God gave me your name last night. I think you know a woman I need to get in touch with. When we locked eyes, I just knew that you were him, the name I had been given, I mean." Jordan cursed her rambling words. Why couldn't she make her words make sense, especially when they mattered so much?

Patrick's blue eyes were ice, sending shivers through her soul as he searched her face. "Sit down and tell me more about this communication from God."

Her mouth fell open. Did he believe her? "I... okay." Their table was square, and as he was sitting across from his daughter, Jordan took the chair to his left and the little girl's right.

He folded his hands on the table as he stared evenly at her. If she wanted him to trust her, she'd better start at the beginning. She spilled out the story, pausing only long enough to let Patrick pray when the waitress returned with their food. Paula shot them all an inquisitive look, but she kept her questions to herself.

"So, let me get this straight. You dropped everything to

come here and find me, or I guess my friend, based on feelings you get?"

Jordan's eyes dropped to the table. He didn't believe her. "Feelings and visions. Sometimes I get visions and sometimes dreams." She mumbled the last few words feeling like a fool for approaching this total stranger.

"It must be nice."

Jordan's eyes popped up. "I'm sorry, what must be?"

"Having that close of a connection with God. I can't remember ever hearing his voice, and so many times I've wondered if I am on the wrong path."

Relief flooded her body. He believed her. "I don't know why He chose me. I wasn't even a believer until a few months ago. It is nice to have a pretty solid idea of what to do, but it's also daunting. What if I don't follow the vision? What if I get it wrong? That's a lot to carry on your shoulders."

"I hadn't thought of it like that." Silence descended then as Patrick ate his breakfast.

Jordan waited, pursing her lips together to keep from hounding him with questions.

When his plate was clean, he laid down his fork and leaned back, crossing his arms. "I know who the woman is, but I can't just give you her information. I believe you are telling the truth, but the information isn't really mine to share."

Jordan's heart sank. Had she come this far only to have to go home empty handed?

"Here's what I will do." He pulled a pen from his pocket and grabbed a clean napkin. "I will ask her to join us for dinner tonight. You can talk to her then, but I will be there too." He scribbled an address down and handed the napkin to Jordan.

A smile broke out on her face as elation filled her soul. "That's fine. That's great. Thank you. Thank you so much."

He nodded. "I'm only doing it because I'm hoping you can help her."

As Jordan stood and tucked the napkin in her pocket, a sobering thought hit her. She might be meeting the girl from her visions tonight, but she had no idea what she was supposed to say to her. It would be a long afternoon spent in prayer.

Having some time to kill, Jordan wandered down towards the capitol building after she left the café. There was a lake at the base of the hill the capitol building sat on, and a gravel path that seemed to encircle the lake.

As she walked, the beauty of the trees and the lush green grass struck her. Though the campus of Tech itself was kept watered and stayed green, the summers in Lubbock were too hot for much of anything else to grow. It was more brown than green, but here the lake was a bright blue and several ducks swam across its surface. The air was warm, but not stifling, and as it was still before noon, there weren't many people out.

She passed a few teens glued to their cell phones and sighed. Technology was great, but it seemed that in the last few years, people were so glued to their phones and social media that no one was out enjoying God's creation. Her feet stopped as inspiration hit her. Were people no longer listening to God because they were so glued to their "idols?" Was that why God was now reaching out to them this way? She glanced down at her watch, wishing the time would speed up. She couldn't wait to meet the mystery woman and share this revelation with her. Surely, she would be as excited about the prospect as Jordan was.

STILL THURSDAY

*K*at closed her laptop for the day and picked up her purse. Patrick had texted a few minutes ago inviting her to dinner, and though she had hoped to make the gym for a workout, she knew Patrick and Maddie needed her.

"Any plans tonight?"

Kat looked up to see Micah in her doorway. Strange how she thought of him as Micah now instead of Dr. Gibson. It must have been the kindness he showed her. He had yet to commit her.

"Yeah, dinner with a friend tonight and then," she sighed, "probably more soul searching." She was still waiting for some answer from God on what she was supposed to do with the lights she kept seeing around people.

"Is it getting any better?" He fell into step beside her as they walked to the elevator.

Better? That was hard to define. She was less angry, but still so confused. However, she hadn't told Micah about the lights, and she didn't feel like getting into that conversation with him now. "Yeah, maybe a little. I'm praying again but still waiting for an answer."

He flashed a crooked smile at her as the elevator door opened. "I bet you won't have to wait much longer."

Kat cocked her head at the cryptic reply. "Aren't you coming?"

"No, I just remembered I still have some work to do." He winked at her as the doors closed.

Kat blinked at the closed doors. Was he hitting on her? Or was she imagining his friendship as more? She shook her head. It didn't matter. Romance was not on her mind right now.

~

Kat pulled into the driveway of Patrick's house and parked the car. She should have asked him if he needed her to bring anything, but since he hadn't asked, she assumed he had dinner planned.

The front door was unlocked, but she knocked on it as

she pushed open the door. It was still weird going in unannounced. "Patrick? I'm here."

"In the kitchen," his voice came back.

Kat continued into the kitchen and stopped short. Was that a girl with him? What was going on? If he was telling her he had met someone already, she might just test out the right cross she had been perfecting on him.

Patrick stood as she entered, but the girl remained seated. With long blond hair and a clear complexion, she resembled a younger Stella, but surely Kat had this all wrong. It was too soon, but what else could this be?

"Hey, Kat," he said, moving to her. "Thanks for coming."

"What's going on, Patrick?"

He cleared his throat and looked back at the pretty blond. "I want you to meet someone."

Kat's shoulders tensed and her hands curled into fists at her side. "What have you done, Patrick?" she seethed through clenched teeth.

"What?" He blinked at her and then the corners of his lips pulled up in a small grin. "No, Kat, it's not like that. Just come and sit down."

She followed him to the table, more confused than ever. If he wasn't seeing this girl, then who was she and why was she here?

"Kat Jenkins, this is Jordan Wright. She flew all the

way out from Texas to meet you." She turned confused eyes on him, and his grin widened.

"To meet me? Why?" Kat sat across from the blond. She couldn't be older than twenty or twenty-one. Her green eyes stared at Kat, but her face remained stoic. She had a light dusting of freckles across her nose and a prominent beauty mark on her cheek.

"Because God told me to."

Even with everything going on in her life, Kat found this hard to believe. People didn't jump on planes and fly out to meet people they didn't know just because of a feeling, did they?

"Hear her out," Patrick said, touching her shoulder as he sat beside her.

"A few weeks ago, I began receiving visions from God," Jordan began. "I didn't know what to do with them, but after praying, I felt compelled to talk to the woman in my vision. I told her the words I had heard in my head–she was on the right track. It meant nothing to me, but it was the sign the woman had been praying for. That woman was my pastor's wife and after hearing my story, she told me I have the gift of prophecy. After that, the visions kept coming, always with some message to pass along to the person. Then a few weeks ago, I saw your face. You stood at a window as the rain fell outside. Your hair was wet, and you seemed sad and angry at the same time."

Kat sat a little straighter at these words. She remembered the moment well as it had been the day of Stella's funeral just before she threw her Bible across the room, but how could this girl she had never met who lived across the country know that?

"A few days later, God showed me a vision of Washington state, and that's how I knew you lived here. Then on my way, I received the capitol building, so I deduced you lived in Olympia. When I landed in Washington, He gave me Patrick's name, and I ran into him this morning over breakfast."

Kat felt like someone had punched her in the gut; the air wouldn't fill her lungs right. Even if she didn't believe this girl, that was a lot of coincidences. Patrick caught her eye and patted her knee, giving encouragement and a silent cue to keep listening at the same time.

"I still didn't know why we were supposed to meet," Jordan continued, "but this morning, I got a vision of you or as you rather, and I saw the light—the light you see around people sometimes."

Kat's jaw dropped, and she whipped her head to stare at Patrick. "Did you tell her about that?" Kat asked.

Patrick's eyes were wide. "No, I didn't know that part until just now either."

"Kat, I know this is a lot to take in, but I think you also have a gift from God. He told me the lights are angels protecting people who need your words."

"But why now?" Kat asked, even as the memory of Dr. Gilead filled her head. Hadn't the doctor said that the light might have been God's way of communicating with her. "I never saw light around people before. I've never had visions. Why all of a sudden?"

Jordan shrugged and shook her head. "I don't have the answer for that. I wasn't even a believer until a few months ago, and I didn't get visions when I first accepted Christ. I have a theory, but it's just a hunch."

Kat wasn't sure if she wanted to hear the theory. There were too many thoughts colliding in her head as it was, but the question tumbled out anyway. "What's your theory?"

"This morning, I was walking around the lake, and I saw people glued to their phones. What if people are no longer taking the time to listen for God's voice and so He has given us these powers to help remind them?"

A silence fell as Patrick and Kat took in that piece of information. Kat thought back over her last few years. Though she wasn't obsessed with her phone, she did always have it with her, and there did always seem to be something that kept her from praying. Some distraction that really wasn't important, but she'd thought it was. She had never heard a voice, but had she ever been silent long enough after praying to have heard a voice?

"It makes sense." Patrick's voice broke the silence. "I can't remember the last time I was still and listened for

God's voice. This could be His way of getting people's attention."

"But why me?" Kat asked. "Why not you? Or the pastor? Or someone with a little more credibility?"

Patrick shook his head and Jordan followed suit.

"I don't pretend to have all the answers," she said. "I'm new at this as well, but after I gave my son up for adoption, I asked God for a purpose. I asked Him to use me, and I think He is."

"But I didn't," Kat protested, and then she stopped. She had asked God to use her, but that had been after the lights. "Well, maybe I did, but I was already seeing the lights by then."

"Didn't you start seeing them shortly after Stella died though?" Patrick said quietly.

Kat nodded, wondering what he was suggesting.

"Maybe God chose you because of that. Maybe He wanted to give you a purpose or a meaning to Stella's death. Maybe you were open even if you didn't know it because you were so hurt." The words were soft, and Patrick's eyes never rose from the table to look at her, but something in them rang true for Kat.

Kat leaned back, letting it all sink in. No one said anything for several minutes. "I'm sorry, this is a lot to take in," Kat said, breaking the silence. "I don't even know what to do with this information."

"It's okay," Jordan said. "It took me a week of the

visions before I responded to them. My suggestion would be to pray. God will give you the answer. I'll be praying as well. I'm staying here locally until I feel like God says I'm done. Here's my cell number." She pulled a piece of paper out of her pocket and slid it across the table.

Kat picked it up, noting the hotel name across the top. The Governor. It was one of the older hotels downtown, but Kat could see why the girl would choose it. It was centrally located downtown and close to a lot of places by walking.

I'll work on that," Kat said. "God and I haven't been on the best of terms lately."

Jordan smiled. "That's okay; He understands that too."

Kat cocked her head as she took in the girl. She seemed much more mature than her face suggested she was. What had happened in her past to grow her up so quickly?

"Well, shall we pause this discussion for dinner?" Patrick asked the two girls.

"Where is Maddie?" Kat asked noticing for the first time that she was not in attendance.

"In her room watching Frozen. Again," Patrick responded with a grin. "I think she'd be interested in this, and if not, she can always play while we chat."

Jordan smiled for the first time and Kat saw years shed off her face.

~

"*A*unt Kat, you have to do it." Maddie bounced up and down, pulling on Kat's hand.

"I don't know, honey," Kat sighed. "It's not really in my comfort zone."

"But God is asking you to." The words came out of Maddie's mouth so matter-of-factly, as if this were the most natural thing in the world and she couldn't believe Kat would even think about not doing it. Then again, it probably was the most natural thing to her.

"Okay, sweetie, I'll think about it. For now, though, how about we get your jammies on? It's late."

Maddie nodded. "But I'm going to pray you do it," she added.

Kat followed Maddie to her room, helped her get into jammies, and read her a story before returning to the living room. Patrick entered, having returned from dropping Jordan off at her hotel, just as Kat sat down on the couch.

"Wine?" He tossed his keys on the coffee table and turned toward the kitchen.

"Sure," Kat agreed, curling her feet beneath her.

There was the soft sound of glasses clinking together, a pause, and then Patrick returned, holding two glasses of red wine.

"Do you think I should do this?" Kat asked, accepting

a glass. She stared into the wine hoping for some clarification, but the red liquid just rippled back and forth like silk.

"I can't tell you what to do," he sat beside her, "but if there's even a chance this is from God, do you want to risk ignoring it?"

Kat took a sip of the warm liquid as she pondered that thought. She was just turning back to God, but did she really want to incur His anger? After all, God sent a storm after Jonah and then he was swallowed by a giant fish. Not that she feared a giant fish today, but what if what Dr. Gilead had said was true? What if more people were affected because she didn't follow God's calling? She couldn't live with herself if that happened.

Kat swirled the liquid gently watching it wash up the side of the glass before cascading back down leaving a trail of red in its wake. She took another sip as if it could imbibe her with courage. "You're right. I guess it wouldn't hurt to just see."

Patrick smiled and squeezed her arm. Warmth spread from the site of his hand, and Kat looked down at it. The air between them crackled in the silence. *What is this?* Kat forced her eyes to Patrick's; his still stared down at the touch as well. When his eyes connected with hers, he pulled his hand away.

"I'm sorry," - he began, but Kat cut him off.

"For what? Nothing happened. However, it's late, and

I should probably be going." She handed him the still nearly full glass and stood up, eyes searching for her purse.

"Kat, you don't have to go…"

"I'm just tired. Long day of work, you know?" Her eyes landed on her bag and she scurried that direction to grab it. She was careful to keep her eyes on the floor because she was afraid of meeting his. Something between them had shifted at that last glance, and she wasn't sure how to deal with it. She wasn't even sure she wanted to deal with it.

"Kat -"

"No, really, it's okay. I'll see you later." Without giving him the opportunity for another word, Kat let herself out of the house and hurried to her car.

Once inside the safety of her small car, she let her mind hash through what had just happened. Was she attracted to Patrick? He was handsome with his clear blue eyes and his copper-colored hair, though she had never seen him that way before. He had always been Stella's Patrick, but now Stella was gone. Was it even okay to fall for your best friend's husband if she was gone? It seemed like there should be rules against that. Maybe it wasn't even attraction. Maybe it was just a connection because of their shared loss. That happened, right? Survivors bonding because of a shared trauma? Surely that was it. Surely there hadn't been any meaning in that touch on her arm. But if it meant nothing why was her arm still tingling?

Why had her heart fluttered in her chest? Why had she wanted him to lean down and kiss her?

Kat pounded her hands on the steering wheel, frustrated. This was not how her life was supposed to go. She was supposed to become a famous doctor and fall in love with an artist. She wasn't supposed to be falling for her best friend's husband, and she certainly wasn't supposed to be seeing light around people or hearing messages from God.

Kat took a few deep breaths to calm her nerves before starting the car and heading home. It didn't stop her mind from racing through all the questions again though.

～

"What was that?" Afriel asked.

"Confusion." Galadriel scanned the area, a scowl on his face. "If demons can confuse human's minds with emotions, they can keep them from focusing on the task at hand. Kat was close to accepting her gift, but now she'll be distracted with this feeling. We'll have to double our efforts. It might be time to really show her."

～

*J*ordan tossed her purse on the bed and looked around the room. The dinner had gone well with Patrick and Kat, or at least as well as could be expected with near strangers, but now she was back in this hotel room alone and lonely.

"I hope we convinced her," she said aloud to the room. If anyone had seen her talking to herself, they would have thought she was crazy. Even Jordan thought she was crazy the first time she talked aloud to God, but there was something about talking to Him like he was in the room with her that comforted her and gave her peace. "It's not like I don't like doing your will, but I am curious how long I'll be staying here."

No audible voice answered, but her phone rang. Jordan dug it out of her pocket, surprised, but pleased to see Jeremy's number on the screen.

"Hello?"

"Hi," he said on the other end. "Are you busy? I thought you could use some conversation."

Jordan looked up at the ceiling and smiled. God always seemed to come through for her. She propped up a pillow and sat on the bed, phone to ear, and listened as Jeremy regaled her with the details of his day. When he had finished, she returned the favor and they talked until her eyes grew heavy. Before nodding off to sleep, she turned the light off, though she never made it out of her clothes.

FRIDAY

Kat woke the next morning with one thought in her mind. She needed to talk to her mother, to tell her what was going on and get her take on it. Her mother had been her rock growing up, and the two women still shared a close relationship when Kat had time. Especially now that her mother was alone again. Kat's father had passed away a year ago.

After dressing, she called work to let them know she'd be late, fired off a text to her mother, ate a quick bite, and headed to her mom's house.

"Kat, are you okay?" her mother asked when they were seated around the table. Her green eyes clouded with worry. "You've lost weight, and you haven't called in weeks. I know you are dealing with Stella's death, but is there more?"

With a sigh, Kat's finger traced an imaginary pattern on the tabletop as she tried to figure out of the right words to say. "I think I might be going insane," she whispered, dragging her eyes up to meet her mother's gaze.

A tiny flicker of something flashed in her mother's eyes, and she sat a little straighter. "What are you talking about?"

"After Stella's death, I started seeing light, Mom. Around people. Not everyone, but people all the same, and yesterday a girl showed up to tell me God sent her from Texas, and she thinks the lights might be angels protecting people I'm supposed to talk to."

"And so it begins again," her mother said as she met Kat's gaze.

"What begins?" Kat asked. "Going crazy?"

"No." Her mother shook her head, sending her raven curls bouncing against her pale cheek. "This isn't the first time you have seen something supernatural, Kat."

Kat narrowed her eyes. "What are you talking about, Mom?"

Her mother's shoulders rose and sank as a large sigh escaped her lips. "When you were two years old, you told me you saw Jesus."

"If I was two, Mom, I was probably just imagining things." Kat wasn't sure she liked where the conversation was going. Suddenly going crazy didn't sound so bad.

"That's what I assumed at first too," her mother said.

"The first time we were on our way to church. I asked you if you loved Jesus, and you nodded. But then you looked up in the corner of the ceiling, waved, and said hi to Jesus. I didn't speculate much about it because you were two and I had just been talking about Jesus but that wasn't the last time."

A chill ran down Kat's back. Her mother really believed this.

"A few nights later as I was putting you to bed, you told me Jesus watched you sleep and then you smiled, waved, and spoke to him again. But it was the third time that really convinced me.

"It was the same week, and we were reading a bedtime story when you climbed out of my lap and walked over to the corner of your room behind the door. You looked up at the ceiling and said, 'hi, Jesus.' Then you tried to give Him your bunny. You held it up and cocked your head as if listening to something. 'No?' you said and then you grabbed a book and did the same thing. You offered four items up, each time tilting your head as if listening. Then you toddled back to me and told me Jesus didn't want your things; he just wanted you to listen."

Kat's mouth parted as she tried to grapple with this story she had never heard. "Why did you never tell me?"

Her mother sighed and shook her head. "I was scared. At first, I thought it was cute and then I wondered if maybe you had a gift, but when I told the story to some friends, they freaked out. They suggested it might be something demonic you were seeing, and it scared me. I asked you the next time it happened what Jesus looked like and you told me He wore white and smiled a lot. It didn't seem like demonic powers would do that, so I was fairly comfortable knowing you weren't going to be possessed, but not knowing what to do with your gift, I let it go. Eventually you grew older and stopped talking about it, and then we stopped going to church and it didn't matter anymore."

Kat reached out and covered her mom's hand. She knew thinking back to the time of her father's affair was hard on her mom. It had been hard on all of them, and it had changed the family. Though he had eventually come back, an air of separation remained in the family, and even when they began attending church again a few years later, it was never with much intensity. Kat hadn't even re-dedicated her life to Jesus until her senior year when a speech at a retreat had touched her.

Her mother squeezed her hand and then regarded Kat once more. "The thing is, Kat. I think you might have a gift. I truly believe you saw and heard God when you were two, and therefore I'm inclined to believe He is trying to get your attention now."

"Why would he want me? I didn't listen when he asked me to pray for Stella. I turned away from him when she died. Yelled, threw my Bible, have barely prayed since."

A small smile tugged on her mother's lips. "You know, I seem to remember there being a story about a man named Saul who was killing Christians, yet God spoke to him and he performed a one-eighty and began preaching."

"I'm no preacher, Mom," Kat shook her head. "I'm a doctor."

"My point is that God uses unexpected things to show his glory. He gives people the ability to do things they would never be able to do on their own so that others will witness those miracles."

Kat sat back and thought about her mother's words. Could she really have some gift like that?

Her mother sighed. "Do you remember the message Pastor Ron spoke on just before Stella's death?"

Kat pursed her lips as she tried to remember. "Something about the Holy Spirit, right?"

"Exactly. It was about surrendering your life to the Holy Spirit. I haven't said anything, Kat, because I wanted you to come to the conclusion, but I wondered if you'd ever really given control of your life to God."

"I accepted him in High school, Mom," Kat said.

"No, I know, but sometimes we accept God without giving over control. We believe He died for our sins, but we don't want to let go of the reins of our lives. I was like that after your father came back. I thought I had forgiven him, but the feelings of anger and hatred kept coming back. It wasn't until years later that I heard a similar sermon and realized I wasn't letting the spirit lead because I wanted to hang on to that anger. When I let God take control, my resentment left and that's when things got better."

Kat stared at the tabletop as she processed the words. Could she let God take complete control of her life? What would this mean for her practice? What was she supposed to do with the lights? "Thanks, Mom. I have to get to work, but I promise I'll keep all of this in mind."

"You can't run from God, Kat." Her mother pulled her in for a hug. "One way or another, He will find you."

Those words rattled in Kat's head as she drove into work that morning.

"I have a message for you," Stephanie said as she passed the reception desk.

Kat stopped and focused on the girl. "What message?"

"I don't know. I didn't open it. It was just on the desk this morning with your name on it."

"Strange. Well, thank you." Kat took the note and smiled at the receptionist, but as she opened the note on the way to her office, confusion and fear blanketed her. The note was blank. What was going on?"

She pushed open her door and was somehow unsurprised to see Micah in her office. He sat with his back to her, but he seemed to know when she arrived. "Good morning, Kat."

"Good morning to you, Micah. May I ask what you are doing in my office?" She walked past him and set her bag down on the floor by her desk.

"Did you get your clarity last night?"

Kat blinked at him. Why was he so focused on her clarity? "Um, I'm not really sure. Why are you so concerned?"

He stood without a word and shut her door. Then he closed the blinds and turned back to her. "Because we are running out of time."

"Time for what?" Unease erupted on Kat's spine and traveled down her back.

"To save them. Now, it's time for you to see."

Suddenly a bright light filled the room. Kat's hand flew to her face to cover her eyes, but she peeked through her fingers. For a moment, Micah Gibson looked the same. Then Kat saw, or thought she saw, him change. A giant pair of wings spread out from his back and a blinding light emanated from him. As quickly as it came, it was gone, and the light disappeared.

"Who... what are you?" Kat backed up until her rear hit the far wall.

"You already know the answer to that, Kat. I'm an angel, and we're at war. The rapture is coming soon, and there are a lot of souls at risk. Those lights you've been seeing are angels. You've been able to see them your whole life, but you had forgotten. I'm sorry that it took Stella's death to reach you, but we need you."

"But your story. You told me you didn't always listen to God."

Micah smiled. "It was someone's story. Just not mine. I needed to connect with you, Kat. Those angels are protecting people who are close to believing, but they need you. You and Jordan. We've brought you together to help save as many as you can."

Kat shook her head. This was more than she could process at the moment. "How do you know about Jordan?"

Micah smiled. "I know because I arranged it. God said she would help you understand your gift. She has one too. The two of you need to work together."

"But I have a job. I'm a doctor."

"This world is not your kingdom. Your kingdom is in Heaven, and your job is to tell people about Jesus. There isn't much time left, Kat. Events are set in motion, and we cannot stop them."

"Am I supposed to just quit? I have patients."

"They will be taken care of, but if you do not help us, these souls may be lost forever."

"Wait, if you're really an angel, how come everyone can see you?"

Micah smiled. "No one can see me but you, Kat. If

you think back to all the interactions we've had, you will notice that no one else ever spoke to me."

"But, we smiled and waved in the hallway."

He nodded. "Yes, and sometimes there were others around who simply thought you were talking to them. At other times, if you had been paying attention, you would have noticed your coworkers shoot you confused glances when that happened. They chalked it up to stress."

Kat closed her eyes and thought back over all their interactions. He was right. She had never seen anyone talk to him. Never heard anyone mention him. She hadn't thought much about it because she was too busy to get involved with office gossip, but now it all made sense. She opened her eyes and took a deep breath. "And Dr. Gilead?"

"Also an angel. You are important, Kat, and we needed to reach you. Now, you have a job to do. Tell Jordan. Invite her to stay with you. Talk to people, especially those being protected. You will not win them all, but you will win many. And you need to find Raven Ryder. She will be important in the next phase."

Kat's head was spinning. "Next phase? What next phase?"

"When the rapture comes, you and Jordan will come home, Kat. Someone will need to carry on. She will not accept you now, but you must plant the seed. She will be protected for she will play a role when you are gone."

"How am I supposed to do all this?" Kat asked.

"Take each person as they come and do it one day at a time for as long as you have left. We believe in you, Kat." With that he opened her door and walked out of her office.

Kat's knees shook as she sank into her chair. Angels were real. And she could see them. She had no idea how to even do what Micah suggested, but she knew her first step. Kat grabbed her bag from the floor and dug in it until she found Jordan's card.

Her hand shook as she reached for her phone, but she managed to punch in the numbers. "Jordan? It's Kat. I'm offering you a room at my place. I think you may be here awhile."

"What do you mean?"

"It's a long story that I don't want to share over the phone, but trust me. I'll pick you up tonight from your hotel and tell you everything then."

~

*K*at pulled in to the gym that evening with her head pounding. The lights had been everywhere today. It was like accepting this mission had opened the floodgates. While Kat didn't see angelic bodies like she had with Micah, she saw the light around many people throughout her day.

Kat grabbed her bag and headed inside, hoping she would get a break from the light, but it was here. Even a light glowed around Jason today.

"Good to see you again."

"Yeah, you too." Kat waited for something to happen. Would it be a voice like she heard with Stephanie? Would she see an angel? When his eyebrow lifted at her, Kat smiled and continued to the dressing room. Maybe it wasn't instantaneous with everyone. Or maybe only Jordan could hear the voice.

As she pulled off her shirt to change, words filled her mind. It wasn't a voice, but a thought. *His life has a purpose.* Kat nodded and continued changing. Then she put her street clothes in her bag and grabbed her gloves. Her heart pounded as she walked back into the big room.

Jason leaned against the back counter and Kat made her way to him. He smiled as she approached.

"I hope you don't think I'm crazy," she said, "but I wanted to tell you that your life has a purpose."

He cocked his head and stared at her. "Why would you tell me that?"

Kat shrugged. "It's a really long story. I'll tell you one day if you want to know, but let's just say I thought you needed to hear it."

His hazel eyes searched her face, but his expression was masked. Kat had no idea what he was thinking. "Well, thank you, I guess."

Kat felt deflated as he walked away. She had figured it would be easier, but the light remained around Jason. Had she failed then?

"Changing your mind about him?"

Kat turned at the cold voice and found herself face to face with the brunette from a few days ago.

"I thought you said your life was too complicated to date him." She crossed her arms and leaned away from Kat.

"I did, and it still is." Kat wasn't sure why she was justifying her actions to this girl, who had been nothing but thorny to her. She took a deep breath and tried another tactic. "I don't think we've been officially introduced. I'm Kat."

The girl looked down at her outstretched hand and then back up at Kat. "I'm Raven, and Jason is mine."

Kat's jaw dropped as the girl walked away from her. How could she possibly reach Raven? The girl had walls up all around her, and Kat had already made a bad impression. With a sigh, Kat joined the class as they lined up. What had she agreed to?

"Hey, don't worry about Raven."

Kat turned to see Lilly beside her. "What do you mean?"

"I heard what she said to you. She's... prickly is the best word I can think of. You get used to her."

Kat sighed. If only it were that easy. But she couldn't just 'get used' to her, she had to 'get' to her.

She did her best to avoid Raven the rest of the class. It wasn't too difficult as she was with the more advanced group. What was harder was avoiding Jason who was her instructor. Thankfully, she must have scared him at least a little because he kept his distance from her. Kat had never been so thankful to have a class end.

When the class was dismissed, she grabbed her bag and scooted out of the gym before anything else could go wrong. Maybe Jordan would have ideas on how to reach this girl because Kat certainly didn't. And why did she have to be important? Why couldn't it be someone she hadn't met or better yet, someone who liked her? Why couldn't it be Lilly? The girl was young, but she was nice.

Even as she thought the words, she knew the answer. God needed someone difficult so that her conversion would affect more people. Kat sighed and turned the car toward Jordan's hotel room. "I hope you'll let me in on your plan, God."

A few minutes later, she pulled up to the hotel and found Jordan waiting out front with her luggage. She had texted her when she left the gym but hadn't expected her to be ready to go.

Kat put the car in park and popped the trunk. Then she got out and helped Jordan load her suitcase.

When they were both back in the car, Jordan asked the

question Kat knew had been on her mind. "What happened?"

Kat shook her head. The incident still felt surreal and unbelievable. "I saw an angel today."

"What?"

"Yeah, I can barely believe it myself. Bright light, wings and all. I guess I haven't been paying attention, so my eyes were opened. He told me you and I had a job to do before the rapture. Jordan, he basically told me to quit my job, so I don't think you're going back to Texas."

Kat tore her eyes from the road long enough to see Jordan bite her lip. It was the first time she had seen anything close to fear on the girl.

"I suppose I knew that," Jordan said finally. "I knew the end had to be coming soon with everything that is happening in the world. So, what's our job?"

"I'm not exactly sure. We're supposed to talk to people and plant the seeds that will lead them to Christ. The hardest part is we must reach this girl named Raven Ryder. Micah told me she's important in the next phase."

"What's the next phase?" Jordan asked.

"I don't know. Whatever happens after we get raptured. I guess we have some studying to do."

"Wow. Rapture. This is real. Okay, so we find her," Jordan said.

"I already found her. Today. She's a girl at my gym. And she hates me."

Jordan chuckled. "Well, God never said winning people over would always be easy. So, we make a plan. We can do this, Kat. We have to."

Kat smiled and nodded. She was glad God had sent Jordan. Alone, she would have felt overwhelmed and definitely out of her element. But somehow, she knew that the two of them would figure this out. They would just have to do as Micah said and take it one day at a time.

he end!

WOULD YOU LEAVE A REVIEW?

As an author, I highly appreciate the feedback I get from my readers. It helps others make an informed decision before buying my book. If you enjoyed this book, please review at your retailer.

Do you like free books? I'm offering a free sample of my next book Free Sample!

ABOUT THE AUTHOR

Lorana Hoopes is an inspirational author originally from Texas but now living in the PNW with her husband and three children. When not writing, she can be seen kickboxing at the gym, singing, or acting on stage. One day, she hopes to retire from teaching and write full time.

If you enjoyed this story, be sure to check out Lorana's other books.

When Love Returns: The first in the Star Lake series. Presley Hays and Brandon Scott were best friends in High School until Morgan entered their town and stole Brandon's heart. Devastated, Presley takes a scholarship to Le Cordon Bleu, but five years later, she is back in Star Lake after a tough breakup. Brandon thought he'd never return to Star Lake after Morgan left him and his daughter Joy, but when his father needs help, he returns home and finds more than he bargained for. Can Presley and Brandon forget past hurts or will their stubborn natures keep them apart forever?

Once Upon a Star: The second book in the Star Lake series. Audrey left Star Lake to pursue acting, but after an unplanned pregnancy her jobs and her money dwindled, leaving her no option except to return home and start over. Blake was the quintessential nerd in high school and was never able to tell Audrey how he felt. Now that he's gained confidence and some muscle, will he finally be able to reveal his feelings? Once Upon a Star will take you back to Christmas in Star Lake. Revisit your favorite characters and meet a few ones in this sweet Christmas read.

Love Conquers All: Lanie Perkins Hall never imagined being divorced at thirty. Nor did she imagine falling for an old friend, but when she runs into Azarius Jacobson, she can't deny the attraction. As they begin to spend more time together, Lanie struggles with the fact Azarius keeps his past a secret. What is he hiding? And will she ever be able to get him to open up? Azarius Jacobson has loved Lanie Perkins Hall from the moment he saw her, but issues from his past have left him guarded. Now that he has another chance with her, will he find the courage to share his life with her? Or will his emotional walls create a barrier that will leave him alone once more? Find out in this heartfelt, emotional third book (stand alone) in the Star Lake series.

Where It All Began: Sandra Baker thought her life was on the right track until she ended up pregnant. Her boyfriend, not wanting the baby, pushes her to have an abortion. After the procedure, Sandra's life falls apart, and she turns to alcohol. Her relationship ends, and she struggles to find meaning in her life. When she meets

Henry Dobbs, a strong Christian man, she begins to wonder if God would accept her. Will she tell Henry her darkest secret? And will she ever be able to forgive herself and find healing? Find out in this emotional love story.

The Power of Prayer: Callie Green thought she had her whole life planned out until her fiance left her at the altar. When her carefully laid plans crumble, she begins to make mistakes at work and engage in uncharacteristic activities. After a mistake nearly costs her her job, she cashes in her honeymoon tickets for some time away. There she meets JD, a charming Christian man who, even though she is not a believer, captures her interest. Before their relationship can deepen, Callie's ex-fiance shows back up in her life and she is forced to choose between Daniel and JD. Who will she choose and how will her choice affect the rest of her life? Find out in this touching novel.

When Hearts Collide: Amanda Adams has always been a Christian, but she's a novice at relationships. When she meets Caleb, her emotions get the best of her and she ignores the sign that something is amiss. Will she find out before it's too late? Jared Masterson is still healing from his girlfriend's strange rejection and disappearance when he meets Amanda. She captivates his heart, but can he save her from making the biggest mistake of her life? A must read for mothers and daughters. Though part of the series and the first of the college spin off series, it is a stand alone book and can be read separately.

A Past Forgiven: Jess Peterson has lived a life of abuse and lost her self worth, but when she is paired with a Christian roommate, she begins to wonder if there is a loving father looking down on her. Her decisions lead her one way, but when she ends up pregnant, she must make some major changes. Chad Michelson is healing from his own past and uses meaningless relationships to hide his pain, but when Jess becomes pregnant, he begins to wonder about the meaning of life. Can he step up and be there for Jess and the baby?

A Father's Love: Maxwell Banks was the ultimate player until he found himself caring for a daughter he didn't know he had. Can he change to become the role model she needs? Alyssa Miller hasn't had the best luck with past relationships, so why is she falling for the one man who is sure to break her heart? Though nearly complete opposites, feelings develop, but can Max really change his philandering ways? Or will one mistake seal his fate forever?

The Heartbeats Trilogy boxed sets: Includes Where It All Began, The Power of Prayer, and A Father's Love

Brush With a Billionaire: Brent just wanted to finish his novel in peace, but when his car breaks down in Sweet Grove, he is forced to deal with a female mechanic and try to get along. Sam thought she had given up on city boys, but when Brent shows up in her shop, she finds herself fighting attraction. Will their stubborn natures keep them apart or can a small town festival bring them together?

Lawfully Matched: Kate Whidby doesn't want to impose on her newly married brother after their parents die, so she accepts a mail order bride offer in the paper. Little does she know the man she intends to marry has a dark past, sending her fleeing into a neighboring town and into Jesse Jenning's life. Jesse never wanted to be in law enforcement, but after a band of robbers kills his fiancee, he dons the badge and swears revenge. Will he find his fiancee's killer? And when Kate flies into his life, will he be able to put his painful past behind him in order to love again?

Lawfully Justified: William Cook enjoyed serving the town, but he enjoyed the money of bounty hunting even more. When an injury threatens his life, will he change his ways to settle down or will his wild spirit always run free? Emma Stewart recently lost her husband and has moved back in with her widowed father. While she likes helping him heal the sick, she wants a family of her own. So no one is more surprised than she is when she falls for William. Can she offer him enough to get him to stay?

Lawfully Redeemed : Dani Higgins was looking for adventure when she joined the K-9 unit, but she never expected her first case to leave her stranded in the snow and pinned under a tree. Nor did she expect to develop feelings for the handsome stranger who cares for her. Will she be able to forget her past and give love another chance?

Calvin Phillips just wanted his brother to turn from drugs, but somehow he ended up smack dab in the middle of a police investigation when he rescued Dani from hypothermia. Will he be able to convince her he's innocent? Even more importantly, will he be able to open his heart and tell her how much he cares? Or will the fact that she's after his brother doom their relationship before it has a chance to start?

The Lawkeeper Trilogy: Includes Lawfully Matched, Lawfully Justified, and Lawfully Redeemed

Her children's early reader chapter book series:

The Wishing Stone #1: Dangerous Dinosaur
http://books2read.com/WishingStone1

The Wishing Stone #2: Dragon Dilemma http://books2read.com/WishingStone2

The Wishing Stone #3: Mesmerizing Mermaids http://books2read.com/wishingstone3

The Wishing Stone #4: Pyramid Puzzle COMING SOON

authorloranahoopes.com
loranahoopes@gmail.com

Made in the USA
Middletown, DE
01 November 2022

13838403R10125